the BALLOON HUNTER

A FOUND NOVEL

HUGH HOWEY
+ELINOR TAYLOR

PLACE
STAMP
HERE

TO:

Interior lettering by Zoey Mikalatos

Story presented as found

Dear Apocalypse,
I'm writing in my capacity as sole survivor to inform you that, despite your best efforts, I'm still here. As you can see, nothing you've thrown at me to date has been enough, and I rather feel you have let yourself down. Try harder.
By my calculations I have enough supplies to last until my 127th year, so might I suggest you shift things up a notch before I die of old age, or boredom, or both?
From this rooftop I raise a vacuum pack of cocktail sausages and a beaker of warm chablis to you. Bonne chance. Bring it on, loser. Bring it on.
I await your response.

Sincerely,
Rita

PLACE STAMP HERE

TO:

Rita,
Your missive landed like a dinner party. So many new people!
I fear that you've sent out hundreds of messages and I've
spotted just these two. How many other survivors know you
better than me? ¨
Supplies are thin here (as am I). I haven't gone out in a
week to look for more food. But maybe your floating
balloons will give me strength. Today the wind was out of
the NW. I wish the internet was still a thing – I'd know how
far a helium party balloon can travel. Or can they just
go on forever?

Please write
again.

–Clayton

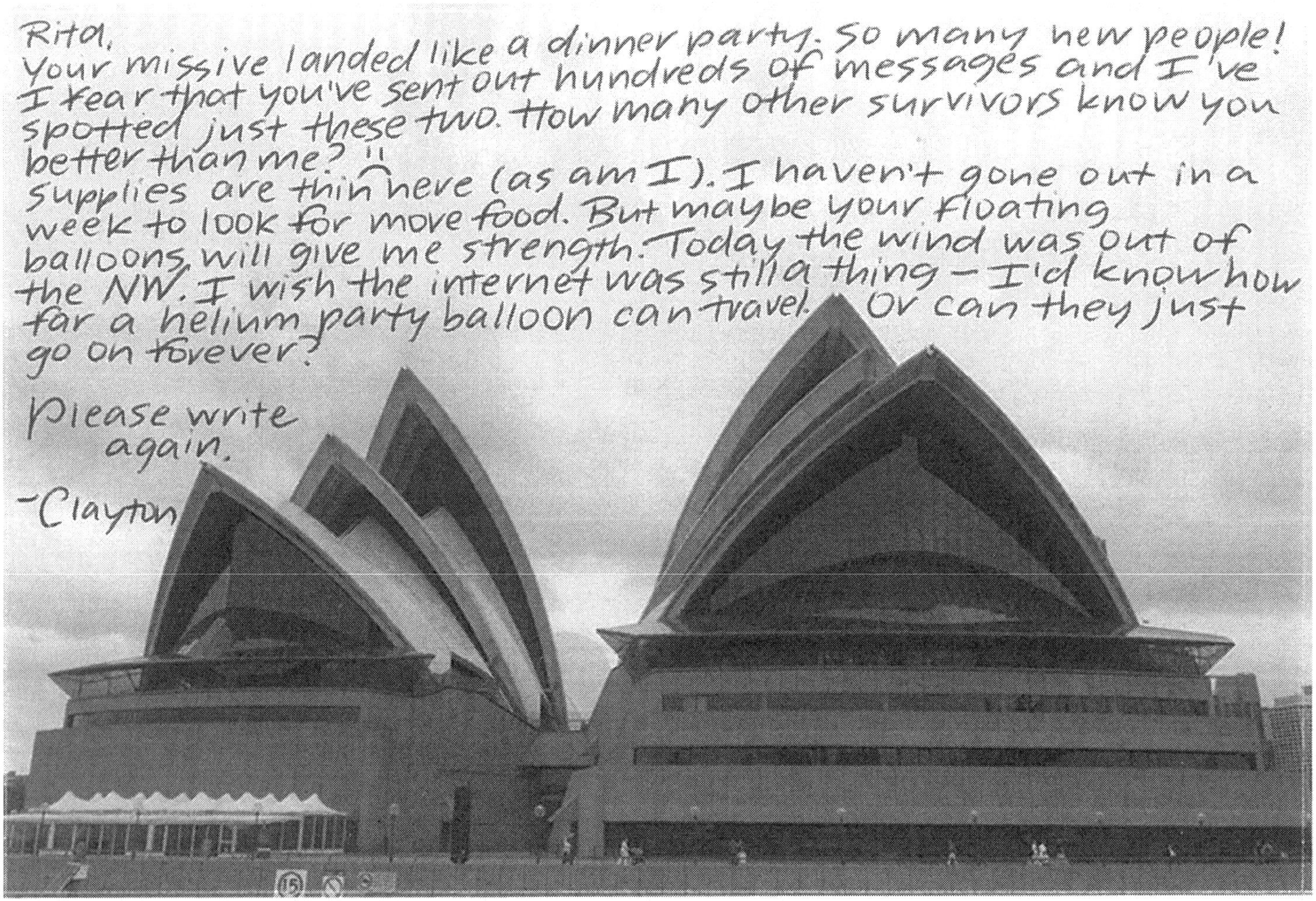

Governor,

Today is an indoor day. Just as most days are now indoor days. The fog rolled back to my corner of the world and will likely stay, as it does, for days.

Thanks for that.

I do not imagine for a second you were unfamiliar with the Law of Unintended Consequences during your time in office, smart as you painted yourself to be. But in any event, if you were around to see it, and I almost wish you were, this would be a good example.

However, the fog isn't the problem. What's in it is.

I didn't vote for this. I didn't vote for you.

Rita

PLACE STAMP HERE

TO:

Rita,
we had a bad bank of fog here two weeks ago. Is that
when you wrote this?
I'm sad to admit that I did vote for that lying sack of
shit. So you're 20, at least. There have been days I wondered
if you were really young or really old. Not sure why
that matters.
I found this message wrapped in a powerline, the balloon
sagging and lifeless. Crawling out along the line, hand
over hand, I thought to myself: with my luck, now will
be when the power comes back.
Of course it didn't. It'll never come back. And I'll
never vote for that asshat ~~again~~ again.

— Clayton

Hey, World,
How are you? You doing okay?
Been a while since I went up to the roof, took a deep breath out there, said hello, what with the fog and all. Sitting tight down here in my shed while it clears, working through a Dan Brown collection. 4.99. Bargain.
Might check outside tomorrow. When the light's right I can see as far as the hills, which must be twenty miles, maybe more. They look different without their usual sprinkling of snow. Do you still do snow? Or shall I add that to the list of lost things?

Regards
Rita

PLACE
STAMP
HERE

TO:

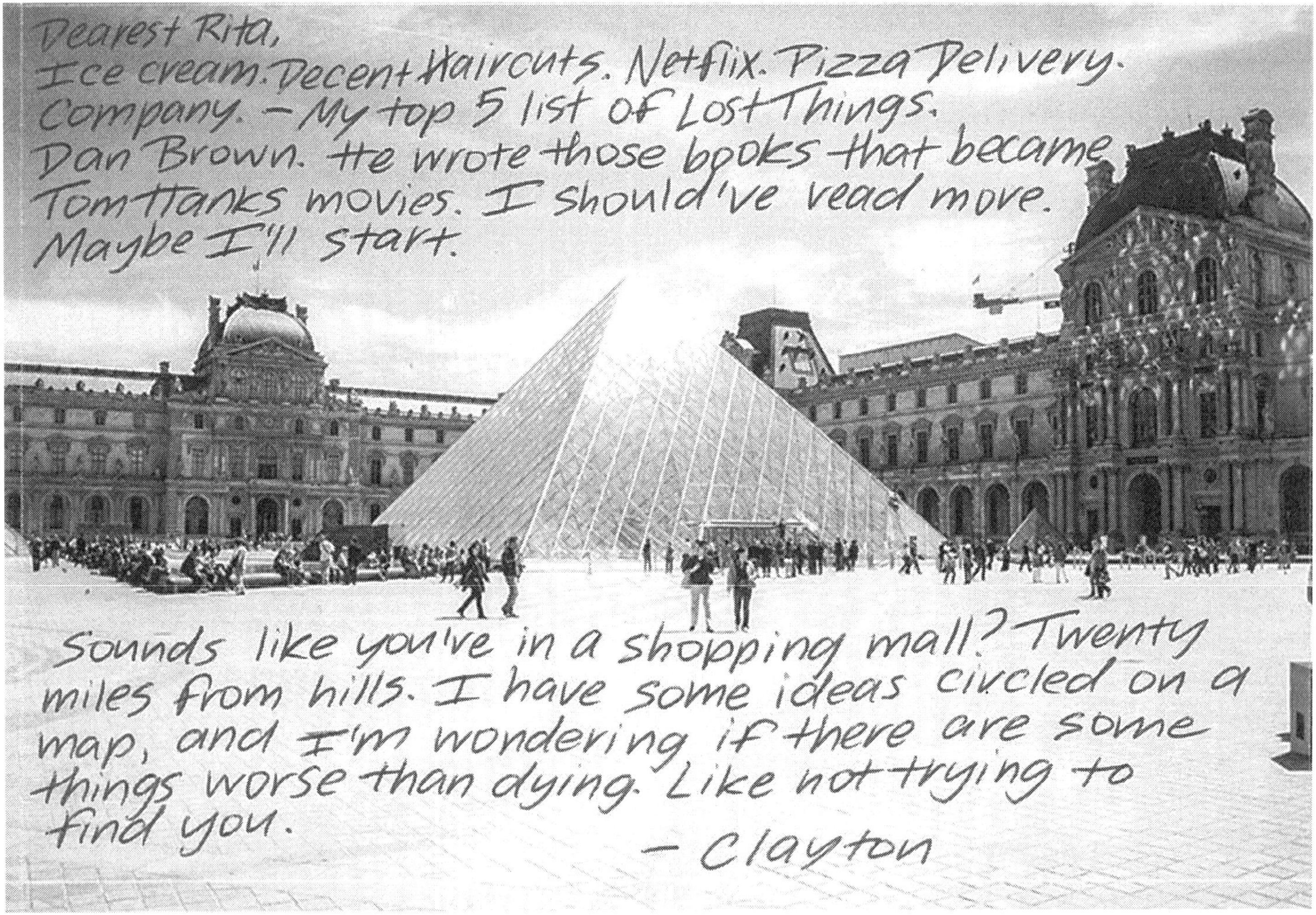

Dearest Rita,
Ice cream. Decent Haircuts. Netflix. Pizza Delivery.
Company. — My top 5 list of Lost Things.
Dan Brown. He wrote those books that became
Tom Hanks movies. I should've read more.
Maybe I'll start.

Sounds like you're in a shopping mall? Twenty
miles from hills. I have some ideas circled on a
map, and I'm wondering if there are some
things worse than dying. Like not trying to
find you.

— Clayton

PLACE
STAMP
HERE

I can't be sure, things got knocked sideways those first few months, but I think today is Christmas. Even if it isn't, I've decided it is. So to celebrate I've cracked open a tinned ham. Frying it up with sprouts and instant mashed potato, and a glass or three of sauvignon blanc. (Second to last aisle before checkouts. Ask me how I know.)

This will be my 100th postcard. Quite some feat, huh? It's definitely 100 as it's the last in the 4th box of 25 that I've floated out into this glorious shitshow of a planet we took for granted.

Is anyone there? Is anyone reading these?

Fuck it. Who cares? It's Christmas.

Rita 

TO:

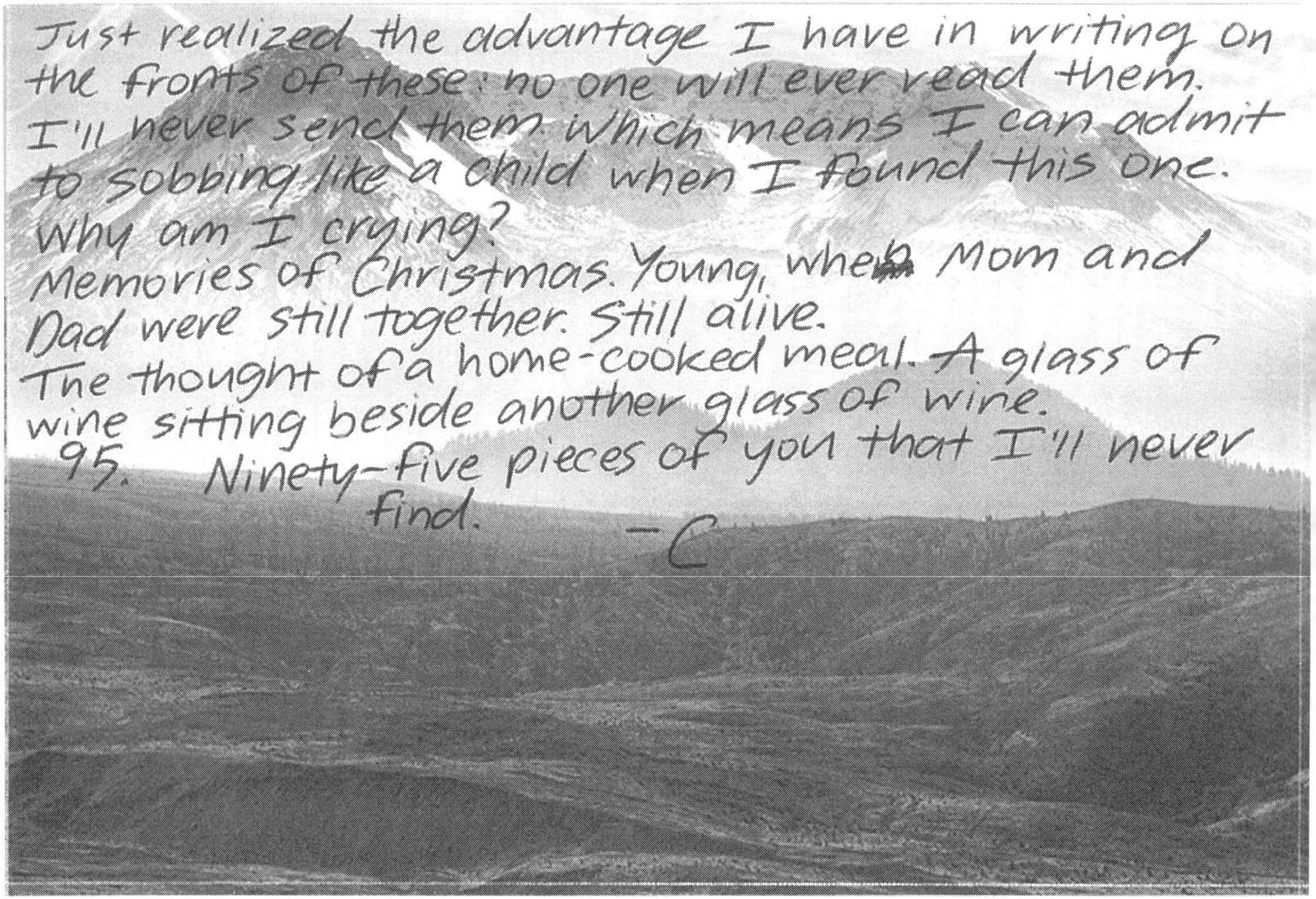

Just realized the advantage I have in writing on the fronts of these: no one will ever read them. I'll never send them which means I can admit to sobbing like a child when I found this one.

Why am I crying?

Memories of Christmas. Young, when Mom and Dad were still together. Still alive.

The thought of a home-cooked meal. A glass of wine sitting beside another glass of wine.

95. Ninety-five pieces of you that I'll never find.

– C

Dear Fog,
Here's the thing: I don't like you. Never have. I suspect the feeling is mutual. You make it easy for things to hide, to sneak around, and this new iteration you've come up with - wow, seriously? Next level creepy.
Also, is it you taunting me with those noises? You know the ones: like whispering voices, or cries.
Once upon a time I might've been happy to pretend it was a fox. Not anymore. I've seen too many corpses, stepped over too many festering flesh heaps, to assume such a harmless source. Everyone is dead. You hear me? Dead.
So, in all sincerity, Fog, take this balloon and shove it.

Rita

PLACE STAMP HERE

TO:

Today is the day I set out. North and West. I'm leaving a lot behind, mostly bad memories. The last of my food only took up half my pack. The rest:

Bedroll.

Two canteens of boiled water.

My Weatherby Mark V.300 (closest thing I have to a best friend).

– Colt Python (never could've afforded one of these in the pre-times).

182 rounds of ammo.

Flashlight.

Knife.

Two Sharpies.

An old tin box that used to hold my wallet, car keys, and wedding ring. Now it's just a handful of postcards. With room for a lot more.

– Clayton

Governor,

I found out something interesting today. One of the dead folks at my place left a newspaper in the staff room and I finally got around to reading it. A few years behind the curve, yes, but still. I was bored of Da Vinci.

You, Governor, took a trip to Florida a week before the climate rocket launch. Tucked away on page five, there you were. Barely news. Shaking hands, all macho pride and teeth, with one of those scientists I used to see on TV, back when there still was TV.

Something about that sits wrong, but I can't quite figure out what it is. It'll come to me. I have time.

Rita

PLACE STAMP HERE

TO:

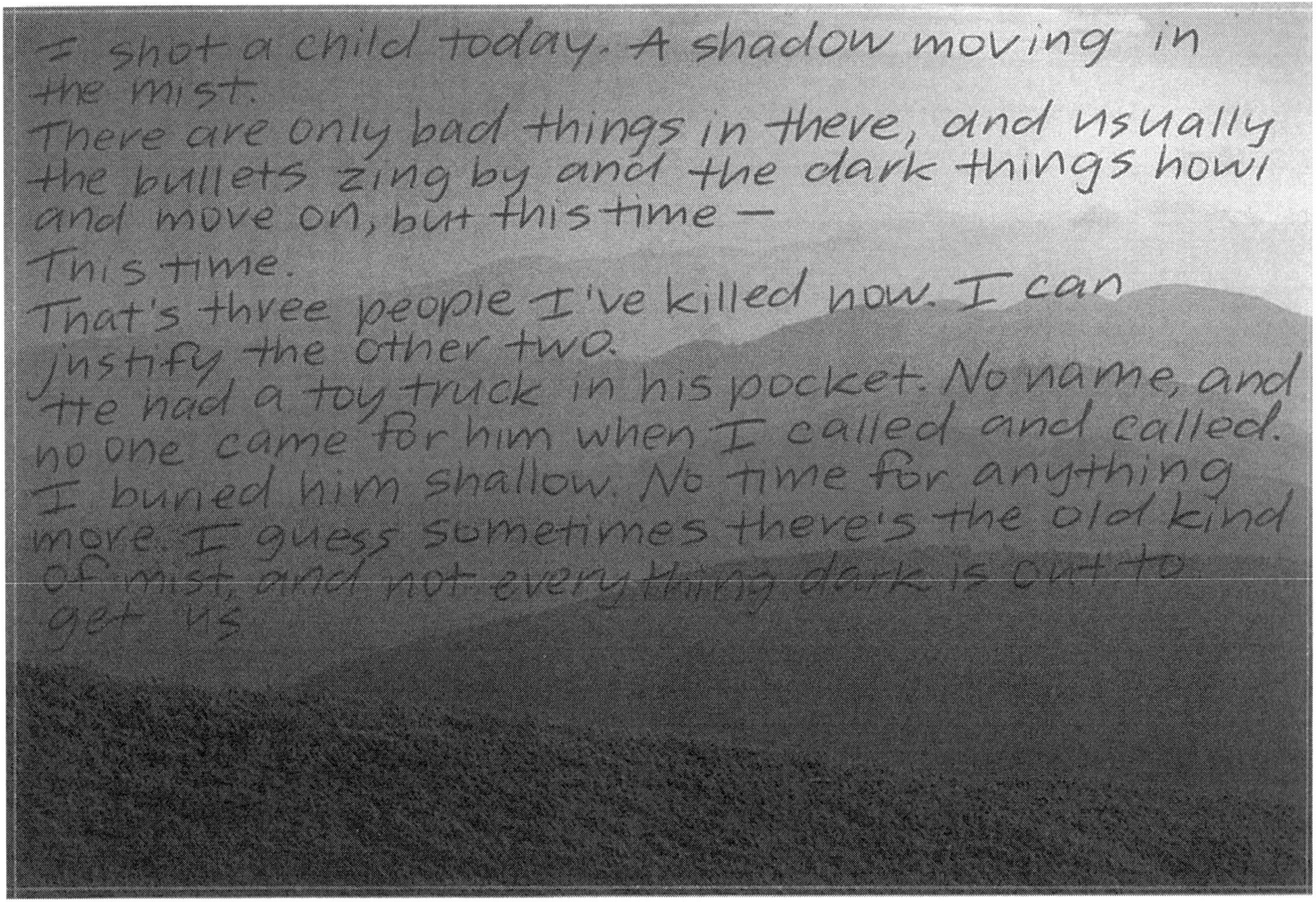
I shot a child today. A shadow moving in the mist.
There are only bad things in there, and usually the bullets zing by and the dark things howl and move on, but this time —
This time.
That's three people I've killed now. I can justify the other two.
He had a toy truck in his pocket. No name, and no one came for him when I called and called.
I buried him shallow. No time for anything more. I guess sometimes there's the old kind of mist, and not everything dark is out to get us

Dear Wes,

I've been thinking about you, today. Every day, truth be told. I know we argued at the wedding, and I'm so sorry about that. It's been playing on my mind quite a lot.

If I'd known the world was turning to shit of course I'd have behaved differently. Any chance we can blame it on the Sambuca? Bygones?

And I was wrong to say Jeannie looked like a sasquatch. She deserved better from me. Family's family. Besides, with hindsight she's definitely more of an orang-utan.

Love you, brother.

Rita

PLACE STAMP HERE

TO:

It's wild watching a neighborhood burn. The flames jump from house to house. No one is here to stop it from spreading, so the wall marches until it hits highway or rain. I wonder if someone starts them on purpose, burning away bad memories? Or is it the lightning?

My Army shrink made me write things down and burn them in a metal bucket, just to practice getting them out there. It was scary. Even if no one would ever read it. Our dark thoughts aren't real if we keep them to ourselves. It's when we utter them that they take shape, become solid, awful things.

I never saw beauty in a flame before, not until I watched those pieces of paper curl up in horror, edges going to ash, recoiling at what they held.

Col. Ramsey. I wonder what she makes of all this. Probably out there making the fog feel bad for being itself.

I would like very much to walk outside, even just circle the perimeter, but I'm afraid. There, I said it. Happy?
I fear death is out there, catching up. That, despite living this long, I could still be infected by it. By death. Is that crazy?
When it gets like my chest might explode I go up to the roof, look beyond the parking lot to a cluster of trees, where at one time squirrels would have scampered, birds nested, before they dropped clean off their branches.
Those trees, those fucking magnificent trees, are surviving better than any of us could. Thriving, actually, in all their verdant glory. I tell myself at least there's that. And it helps a little.

Rita

PLACE
STAMP
HERE

TO:

The pen trembles. I think it knows what I might write if I'm not careful. And it knows I wouldn't dare burn those words away if I put them on one of these postcards.

These postcards mean too much. Too much.

I'm finding them more easily now. Are they calling to me now? Or is my brain just getting better and better at spotting them? I never thought to look up before.

I wake up some mornings and the words aren't real, just an imaginary friend, voices from the fog. But then I touch them, flip through them, and I'm not crazy.

Not crazy.

A confession is welling up inside me, but I'm so scared. More scared of this than anything in the fog.

Five things I miss:

1. Hot running water.
2. Google.
3. The feel of grass underfoot.
4. Eating popcorn in a dark movie theater.
5. Hope.

Five things I don't:

1. Monday mornings.
2. Fox News.
3. Existential dread.
4. Covid.
5. Mike. (Christ, what does that say about us?)

Rita

PLACE STAMP HERE

TO:

I dated a girl named Hope once, back before I enlisted. I used to think it was such a silly name. A hippy name. I got overseas and things faded between us,
and the other kind of hope faded too. What the fuck were we fighting for? All the time I spent being afraid back when there was nothing to fear.
Anyway, it's funny that you end both lists with four-letter names. Hope as a cuss word. Mike as a swear. Fuck them both.

To anyone or no-one,

I'm up to twenty postcards a day and still nothing. No contact. Even the fog has stayed away of late. Thankful for that, at least.

The first helium tank is down to half. I have an abundance of balloons and cards (this place must've had a sale on them or something) but once the gas goes, that'll be the end of that. I've checked the warehouse: two more tanks.

This morning, a light breeze carries my words in the direction of Farley County. Maybe someone made it over there, kept safe down the mines. Maybe not.

Do I want to know the answer either way?

Rita

PLACE STAMP HERE

TO:

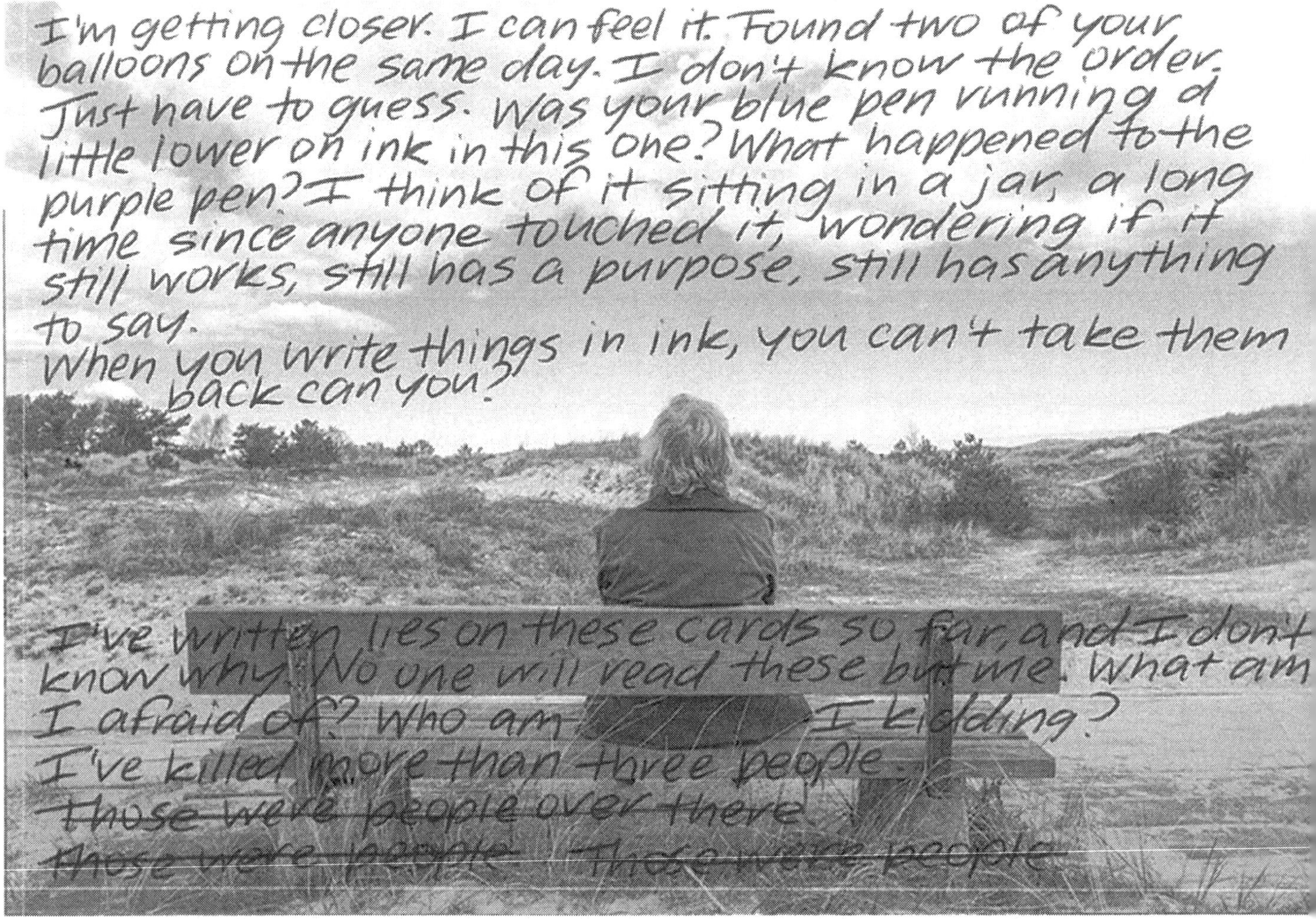
I'm getting closer. I can feel it. Found two of your balloons on the same day. I don't know the order. Just have to guess. Was your blue pen running a little lower on ink in this one? What happened to the purple pen? I think of it sitting in a jar, a long time since anyone touched it, wondering if it still works, still has a purpose, still has anything to say.
When you write things in ink, you can't take them back can you?
I've written lies on these cards so far, and I don't know why. No one will read these but me. What am I afraid of? Who am I kidding?
I've killed more than three people.
~~Those were people over there~~
~~Those were people~~ ~~Those were people~~

Hey, folks,

What are you doing RIGHT NOW? Wanna join me for a party at mine? Sure you do.

Free booze and snacks, giant Jenga, non-stop hits from the 80's and 90's, mostly power ballads and guitar rock, which, full disclosure, may descend into karaoke.

You have been warned.

Dancing in underwear compulsory. Absolutely NO climate crisis talk allowed.

Just knock.

Your buddy,
Rita

P.S. Bring weed.

PLACE STAMP HERE

TO:

FUCK YES! power ballads and jenga? That's a perfect date right there. Trying to imagine you dancing around in your underwear... and I almost don't want to make you out to be prettier than you are. I try not to care. Sometimes I worry that if I find you I'll just spontaneously combust. The longing is too much. Yesterday got a little hairy, a reminder that looking for you will probably be the end of me. But hey, I would've starved to death if I'd stayed put. The end is coming for all of us.

But there was a moment, when the fog had me cornered in this old neighborhood, and it started pushing through the broken windows and up the stairs, and looking for me in the attic... a moment there when I was out on the roof, waiting for it to climb just a few feet more and claim my sorry ass, that I wondered what the hell was it all for, this life? This running around in circles. This pretending to be what I'm not.

I laughed when I realized I wasn't gonna die. The joke's on me. One punchline after another, until I'm black and blue.

This is my first time writing in a while. Though I don't suppose it makes any difference if I leave it a day, a month, a year. Sooner or later I must face the fact I'm alone.

Current status is I've not had a drink since getting full-throttle wasted the other night. I woke up cold, like an idiot, in the electrical items section (also known as: the useless junk aisle). Guess I passed out. Only through blind luck did I not stumble outside.

The noises have started up again these past few nights. If I can cope with the stench, I might check the dead guys upstairs for a gun.

Rita

PLACE
STAMP
HERE

TO:

I live three lives, and I don't know which one to write about.
There's the life of me on the road, looking for a place to sleep each night, looking for cans of food in strangers' houses, taking a shit in a toilet that won't flush, but hey I won't be here tomorrow so who gives a fuck?
There's the life I used to live which feels like a forgotten dream these days. A world of alarm clocks, traffic, deployment, shaving, worrying about how I smelled.
And a fantasy life where I escape the other two. A life with you, a stranger who sends thoughts out above the fog. Where I teach you how to hold a gun and you teach me how to dance. Where we leave notes to each other to find day after day as we grow old and all the four letter names fade. Fade like ink. Even the indelible things we've done... forgotten eventually.

Some day.

Greeting from the birthday girl,

Turns out 36 feels much the same as 35. Does it even matter? If time and age are irrelevant to a life in isolation, so must be the landmarks of womanhood. Before this, my body was a ticking clock. Days collected into a series of repeating patterns.

1-5 Bleed.

12-14 Ovulate.

28 Pregnant?

1 Nope. Start again.

My husband is gone. My body, and my world, no longer move to the same rhythmic beat.

Who even am I now?

Rita

PLACE STAMP HERE

TO:

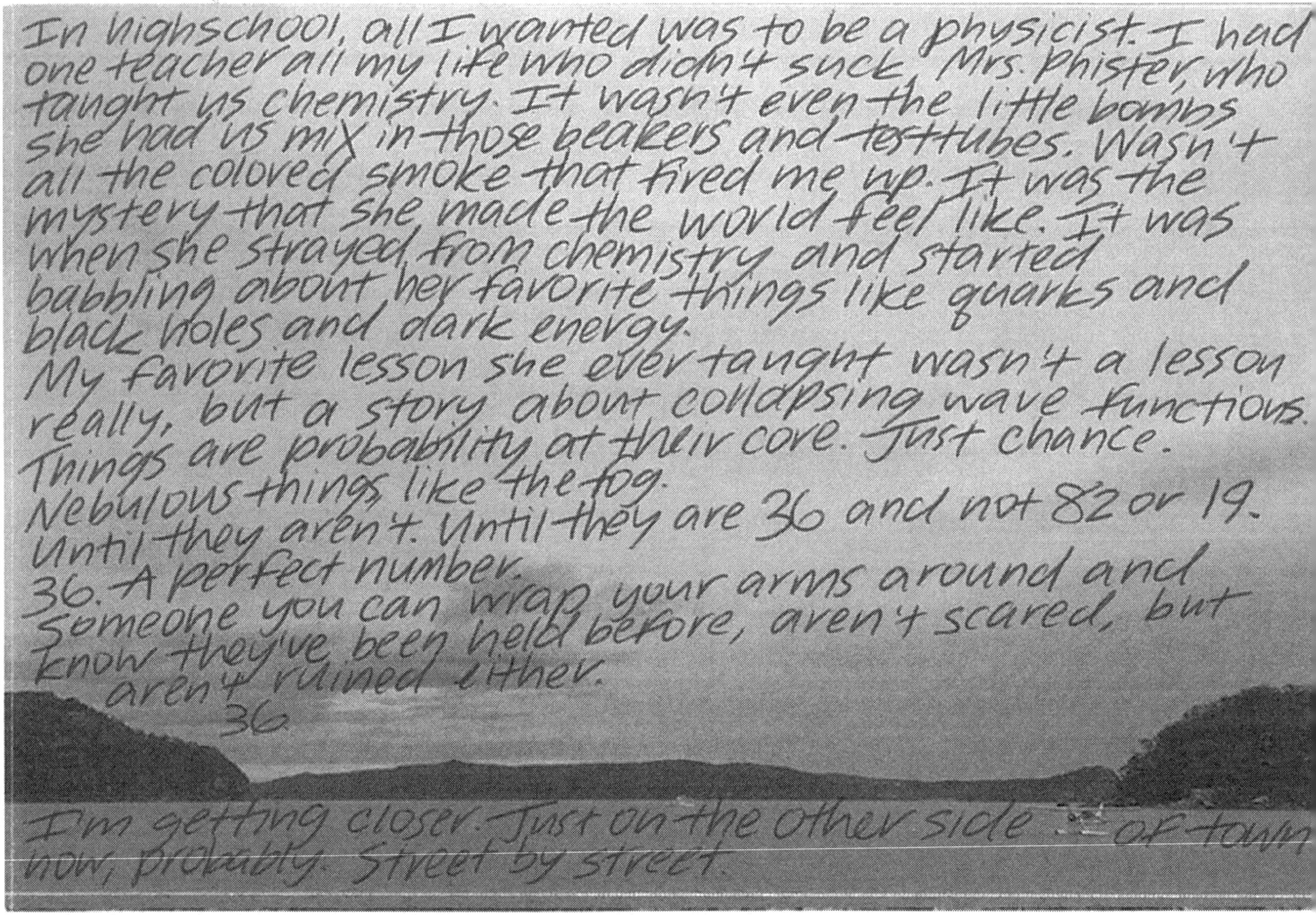

In highschool, all I wanted was to be a physicist. I had one teacher all my life who didn't suck, Mrs. Phister, who taught us chemistry. It wasn't even the little bombs she had us mix in those beakers and testtubes. Wasn't all the colored smoke that fired me up. It was the mystery that she made the world feel like. It was when she strayed from chemistry and started babbling about her favorite things like quarks and black holes and dark energy.

My favorite lesson she ever taught wasn't a lesson really, but a story about collapsing wave functions. Things are probability at their core. Just chance. Nebulous things like the fog. Until they aren't. Until they are 36 and not 82 or 19.

36. A perfect number.

Someone you can wrap your arms around and know they've been held before, aren't scared, but aren't ruined either.

36

I'm getting closer. Just on the other side of town now, probably. Street by street.

I've lost track. Took my eye off the ball and cannot for the life of me remember how many sleeps have passed since I last crossed the calendar.
So I've done away with the old system, declared every day Ritaday.
And, as everyone (me) knows, Ritaday mornings are good for one thing: time trials!
Damn near broke my neck pulling down a BMX from the central display, but totally worth it, as the course I've designed around the store is freaking AWESOME.
All challengers welcome...

Rita
BMX champion
of the world

PLACE
STAMP
HERE

TO:

Another lie on my last note. Too many to keep up with. It wasn't collapsing wave functions that I loved the most. It was that dark energy.

The idea that there's something in the universe trying to tear it all apart. Something that pushes things away inexplicably fast. Something that no one can find, no matter how hard they look.

All that resonated with me.

Dark energy.

It's right here, all you asshole scientists.

I can feel it in me.

Lately I've taken to watching these balloons disappear across the horizon, or until they're swallowed by the haze above, whichever comes sooner, the wind being the deciding factor in that.

I have a telescope. It's one of my most prized possessions. Powerful thing it is, too.

If there were stars to be seen I'd surely be looking up. Instead, I follow my balloons, with their bright, incongruously joyful messages - Happy Birthday! Congrats! It's a Boy! - and their dangling postcard payloads, until I can't see them anymore. What happens to them after that, I can only wonder.

Rita

PLACE
STAMP
HERE

TO:

____

____

____

I'll tell you what happens to them. I shoot them out of the sky or I climb a tree to retrieve them. I fish them out of gutters hoping the ink didn't run so bad I can't make out every word. They get read six times end to end right off the bat, hands trembling with excitement. Then they're flipped over to check out the backs, see how a response might fit.

They go in a tin box that's not as empty as it once was. A perfect fit. Like a hand in a hand. You might think they're nothing, but they are everything.

Memorized. Pored over.

Maybe I'm losing my mind, and these scattered balloons are the evidence.

Or maybe I'm finding myself for the first time.

Negative: I'm not alone. Something has been at the spoiled crackers in the snacks aisle. A mouse, or worse, a rat, probably. Where there is one there are likely hundreds.

Fuck, fuck, fuck.

Sure I saw traps around here somewhere.

Positive: Looks like the sun is trying to break through the ever-present atmospheric haze. Hello, old friend. Long time no see.

Rita

PLACE STAMP HERE

TO:

Rita,
It occurred to me yesterday that sitting still might be harder than being on the move. My body is getting stronger from the walking, from climbing onto rooftops for a better view, from making sure I don't get cornered by the fog or anything in it.
I used to think that you had it all in your big store full of everything and I was out here with nothing. But maybe it's the other way around? Maybe I won't get there and feel rescued, but I'll be rescuing you. We'll find a car that still runs, some way to fix the gas, or charge up one of these treehugger Teslas that're laying about. And we'll just GO you and me.

PS. Found more rounds for the rifle. Makes up for the ones I went through last week.
PPS. Best part of staying on the move is not worrying about everything I leave behind.
PPS. [redacted]

I finally moved a few of the bodies. Didn't have to, it's not like they were anywhere I had to go, but knowing they were there was starting to freak me out, what with the noises and everything. They had employee badges, so we're on first name terms now. wearing rubber gloves, a towel around my nose and mouth, I wrapped Tomasz, Steve, Lenny, and Jerome, (who thankfully folded up more compactly than they would've alive), in individual garden waste bags.

The store has a wheelchair, which is just as well. Those guys are heavy!

One at a time I wheeled them up the access ramp, then threw them off the roof, by the warehouse entrance. I never look in that direction. From 40 feet up, it shouldn't smell.

A good day's work, all in all.

More to do tomorrow.

Rita

PLACE STAMP HERE

TO:

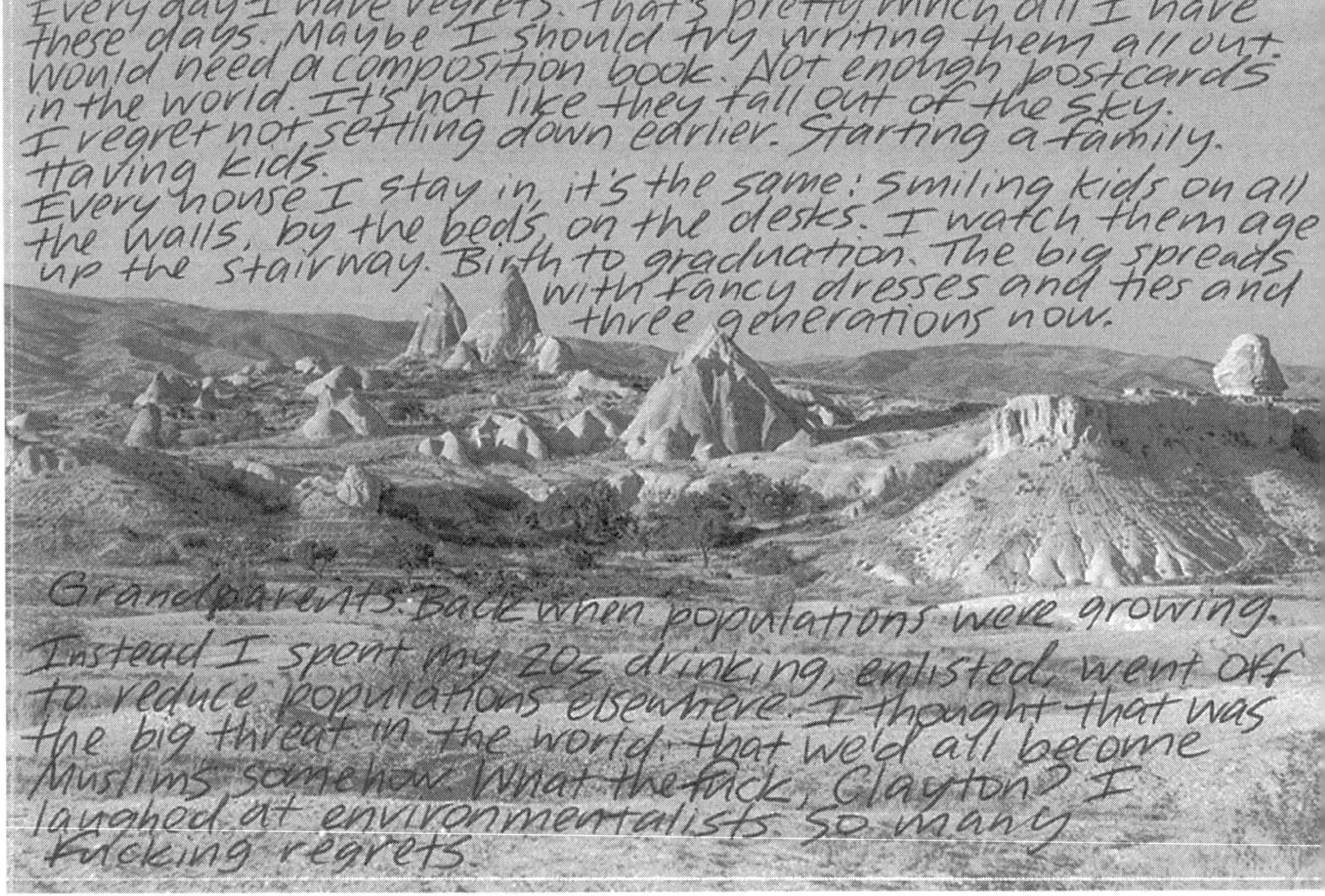

Every day I have regrets. That's pretty much all I have these days. Maybe I should try writing them all out. Would need a composition book. Not enough postcards in the world. It's not like they fall out of the sky.
I regret not settling down earlier. Starting a family. Having kids.
Every house I stay in, it's the same: smiling kids on all the walls, by the beds, on the desks. I watch them age up the stairway. Birth to graduation. The big spreads with fancy dresses and ties and three generations now.
Grandparents. Back when populations were growing.
Instead I spent my 20s drinking, enlisted, went off to reduce populations elsewhere. I thought that was the big threat in the world, that we'd all become Muslims somehow. What the fuck, Clayton? I laughed at environmentalists. So many fucking regrets.

Oh God.
Something, or someone, is coming into the store at night.
Not the warehouse (which, while still terrifying,
wouldn't be as bad, given there's a lockable sliding
door I can close to that) but the main area of the
store. Where I sleep.
I thought it was vermin, but I was wrong.
Whatever it is clawed a hole in the outer wall big enough to
crawl through. I've stacked crates loaded with cans in front
of it for now, heavy stuff, hard to move. I'll figure out a more
permanent solution when I eventually calm down.
Jesus, what next??

Rita

PLACE
STAMP
HERE

TO:

Rita,
So you've got them there too. I want to feel afraid for you. I really do. Mostly I feel an empty pit in my stomach. Part of me hoped that when I got there, we'd be safe. No more shooting at dark things in the mist. No more bodies. None of their howls. But I guess nowhere is safe. Only on the move, staying just ahead. The Army trained us for this, and it's kept me alive so far. But here's another confession written in ink: Part of me was hoping you'd be my savior, not the other way around. It sounds so good where you are. There's a shopping mall another five klicks NW of here that seems a likely target. Five klicks. I used to jog that before breakfast. Every block is a freakin' nightmare. ~~And~~ every bed I sleep in, I almost want to stay there forever.

† Moving is hard.

Time to move.

Dear Mike,
It's rained here for a solid week, and my mind is playing tricks, telling me I didn't cover you with enough rocks to weigh you down.

PLACE STAMP HERE

I had a nightmare: the meltwater from the mountains flushed you out and you came looking for me, majorly pissed off.
You kept repeating the same things, over and over: "I'm cold, Rita", and "Hold me", and "Why would you do that to me?"
I screamed myself awake, then hid under the blankets until morning came.
Stay dead, Mike. Please.

Rita

TO:

It just occurred to me today that people around the world might be dealing with the same bullshit. Houses whose doors I kicked down in Kabul, someone else is kicking that door down right now to find a place to sleep, to hold back the mist, looking at pictures of someone else's family, rummaging for food.
The first time I got on a plane to see another country, it was to shoot the kids who lived there. Felt right at the moment. My god, I thought I was a fucking hero saving the world. Keeping America safe. I thought those people were dangerous. Muslims were gonna take over the world. Used to make fun of people afraid of the ocean because they saw Jaws once. Meanwhile, I grew up playing with my GI Joes.

It's amazing the range of things you find here. My top 5 so far:

PLACE
STAMP
HERE

1. Celestron Refractor Telescope.
2. 22" Kettle Barbecue With Cart (tons of charcoal in store).
3. Lay-Z-Spa Inflatable 4 Person Spa (with multipurpose chlorine tablets).
4. Brita Water Filter & spare cartridges.
5. Kayak.

I was wrong about not being able to smell the bodies from the roof. Might have to do something about that.

Rita

TO:

It's wild that we both make top 5 lists, not top 10. Lack of imagination? Don't think we deserve more? Attention span problems? What does this say about us?
I've always done things in fives. Five years is how long any relationship of mine lasts. How long before the Army got sick of me. How long it took me to get through college. Always things in fives.
This is my slow-ass way of mentioning that I'm down a finger on my right hand. Wish I had a "monster-bit-it-off" story, and maybe one day I will, but it was a stupid accident.

Breaking and entering is an artform. Even with a lot of practice, I still don't have it down.

Weather is not complying either. Might have to sit tight for a few days more.
What the fuck did they do to the air?

Guys!
It's official, I'm a goddamn genius.
Honestly, I'd already impressed myself by fixing up a tarp to a length of hose to collect rainwater in my inflatable rooftop spa. After the recent storms it's filling nicely. Just cold.
How do you heat large amounts of water without electricity for a heater pump? You might well ask.
One word: thermosyphon.
Coiled copper pipe + metal brazier + hose = instant hot water, flowing into my (now) hot tub! God, I'm good at this.
In your face, Apocalypse.

Rita

PLACE STAMP HERE

TO:

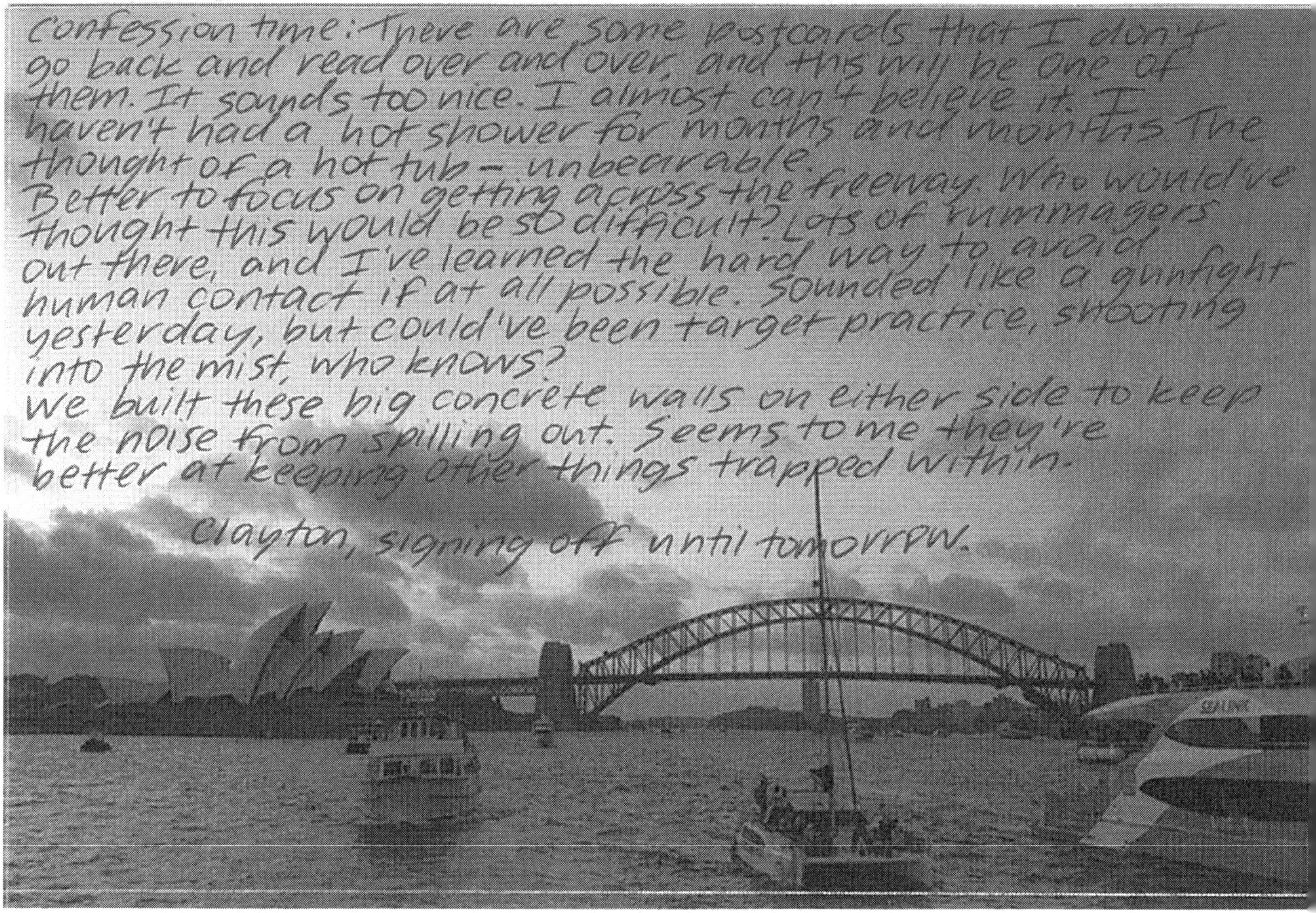

Confession time: There are some postcards that I don't go back and read over and over, and this will be one of them. It sounds too nice. I almost can't believe it. I haven't had a hot shower for months and months. The thought of a hot tub – unbearable.
Better to focus on getting across the freeway. Who would've thought this would be so difficult? Lots of rummagers out there, and I've learned the hard way to avoid human contact if at all possible. Sounded like a gunfight yesterday, but could've been target practice, shooting into the mist, who knows?
We built these big concrete walls on either side to keep the noise from spilling out. Seems to me they're better at keeping other things trapped within.

Clayton, signing off until tomorrow.

I've started locking myself in the shed at night. The time is fast approaching when I decamp to the staff room upstairs, which will at least put one more door between me and the shop floor.

For now, though, I'll make do with the heavy duty bike lock I'm using for home security.

In a bid to soothe my frazzled nerves I'm listening to Jane Austen audio CDs, through headphones, as I drop off to sleep. Been a while since I played anything out loud. Don't want to draw attention.

I'm either being watched or I'm losing it. Take your pick.

Rita

PLACE
STAMP
HERE

TO:

Fuck you, whoever finds this.
Especially if it's the asshole who got me.
This will be my last entry. The last thing I ever write. My
big middle finger to fate and God and the big lie that life
has a grand plan for us all.
So much blood. It doesn't hurt as much as I'd thought,
getting ki So don't take any satisfaction, you
dickheads. Got two of your friends.
Fuck, this is like the plane going down, time
to really think about what's coming, and
you don't have anything good to say.
Or anyone to say it to.

Dear Wes,
Remind me. The weekend before you and Jeannie got hitched, we met for breakfast, remember? We talked about the government's plans for the rocket launch. You had eggs Benedict, as you always do, I had cream cheese bagel and lox.
Had they approved it by then? The launch, I mean. Or did they push it through early? I'm sure there was something... God, my memory is shot to shit, my perception of time like ice-cream melting in the sun.
This is all so wrong. A puzzle with pieces missing.
Come on, Rita, think. THINK!!

PLACE
STAMP
HERE

TO:

Two weeks. I'm tempted to burn the last postcard.
Pathetic. Gonna chalk that one up to my body being in shock. Really didn't think I'd make it, but damn our bodies are tougher than we realize.
Found the convenience store those assholes were using as their home base. And half a dozen of your postcards. Makes me even gladder that I got three of them (found another one here who bled out). The last guy must've tucked tail. Or did I wing him too?
Holy shit, I thought they ended me, but maybe I was their boogie man. Crazy perspective.
Anyway, I found why they'd been ranging out. A goddamn bottle of helium. I think they were trying to send you a message.
Hope that fourth guy is dead. And dammit Rita, what are you thinking with these damn balloons?
There are crazy people out here.

Crap.
The bodies have gone from the warehouse entrance where I dumped them.
Nine corpses. Gone.
I don't know what to do with that information.

Rita

PLACE STAMP HERE

TO:

Launched my first message to you this morning. Wind slightly out of the south. Still not feeling well enough to push that way myself, but a lone orange balloon is making its way. I sent a greeting card. Impossible to think you'll find it. I'm sending out a dozen duplicates, just in case. A little introduction. And if anyone else finds it, good. Let them know I'm still here. Still coming. Still dangerous.

Interesting observation: I've untied dozens of your notes from dozens of balloons, and I had a hard time trying to decide what kind of knot to make. In my rush to get them free, I never once paid attention to how they were assembled.

Got me thinking: how often do we tear things down in such a rush that we have no idea how they were made?

Hello there,

Not sure we've met, but allow me to introduce myself:
I'm Rita Stomhold, fuck up of the highest order, and as I write this I'm doing tequila slammers with a storeful of ghosts.

PLACE
STAMP
HERE

Yes, you read that right. Tequila slammers.
I've set them all out in a row, cracked open a jar of preserved lemons, a dish of salt, and - BAM! BAM! BAM! - down the hatch they go.
Nobody tell me I don't know how to live.
Of course the ghosts are struggling with theirs, so I'm giving them a teensy weensy bit of assistance. They don't seem to mind.

Adios muchachos...
Rita

TO:

May have spoke too soon about pulling through.
Pretty sure the exit wound is infected.
Subsisting on junk food the past week hasn't
helped. If I don't die from abscess,
pretty sure diabetes will get me.
Top 5 things I wish I'd known sooner in life:

1) Drugs aren't all bad. I mean, some of them
are really, really good.
2) The people on TV trying to make us all mad didn't
really give a fuck about anything.
3) Craft beers really do taste better. Even warm.
4) Cuddling is better than sex. I don't care what
anyone says. Or if it makes me homo or
whatever. Right now, just a person to rest my head on.
I'd kill for that.
5) Disinfect, disinfect, disinfect.

Governor,

For a year and a half I slept in a plastic shed. When I shut my eyes I couldn't bear the feeling of vastness around me. I needed to close it in, make it small. The clicks and scratches and trickles that punctuate the silent darkness conjured the worst imaginable things to mind. At night, space was - still is - my enemy.

Did they usher you to a safe place when the sky went dark? To a floating, lead-lined palace, a bunker with servants to spare? Or did some righteous soul, knowing what you did, slip a knife between your ribs?

Because if they didn't, I will.

Rita

PLACE STAMP HERE

TO:

A routine is setting in, and that's worse than gangrene. Routines are murder. Gotta shake this soon.

But until the supplies run out, it's me changing bandages, cleaning a wound that I'm getting to know intimately like a damned wife, sampling candy bars I was too scared to stray from Snickers for, getting drunk on warm beer, and sending up party balloons with greeting cards and tourist postcards attached.

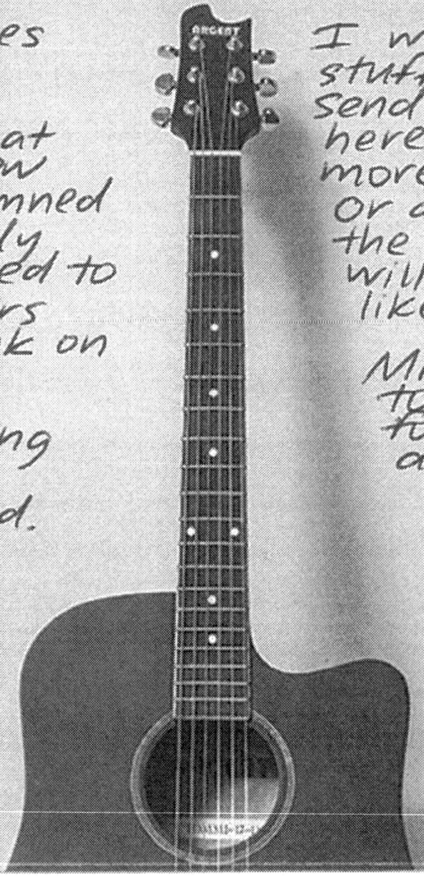

I write all the good stuff on the ones I send out. I think these here are becoming more like a journal. Or a diary. Maybe the real confessions will start spilling out, like yellow puss.

Might need [illegible] to find a new tin for these. One with a lock.

If I've realized one thing over the last few weeks, it's that I need to get my shit together if I'm to stand any chance of getting through this.
I already have everything I need:
My dad's focus, my mother's inner strength, Mike's self-belief, and my baby brother's optimism. I just need to harness them.
So. Yoga. I've taken up Yoga. Or pilates. (No clue what the difference is). I've cleared a space in what was the cafe, laid down foam jigsaw mats, and am spending 30 minutes each morning impersonating what I picture a Yoga instructor to be. Day 3, and feeling more zen already.
Bring it.

Rita

PLACE STAMP HERE

TO:

Here it goes:
First person I killed, I loved it.
Fuck, just seeing that out there, outside of my brain. It's not good. It's really not good. But it's real. And I've lived with it for a long time. And somehow I've known it was a part of me.
I used to worry it meant I was sick in the head, like the kind of guy who could go on a killing spree. They make you see someone after you have an "event." Talk it through. Make sure you're okay. And I don't think I'm the only one who had to pretend like it was traumatic, just to throw them off of the scent.
Can't be the only one.

But it was more than I thought, and I didn't learn that until I killed someone by accident here at home.

Not enough room. I'll wait until I find another postcard. They're thick around here. I know I'm close.

My sleep has improved since moving up to the old staff room. I scrubbed the place raw with bleach, to get rid of the cadaver stink from Tomasz et al. Then again with apple antibac surface cleaner, to cover the smell of the bleach. I've set up a makeshift bed using stacks of outdoor furniture cushions, Egyptian cotton sheets, and a king sized comforter. It's like a little corner of Heaven up there. The space is great. It's bright, with windows (windows!) facing south and east. What we'd call in the good old days 'dual aspect'. During the night, I wrap a length of coaxial cable around the handles of the double doors, holding them shut, to be safe. The fog is back. Can't be too careful.

Rita

PLACE STAMP HERE

TO:

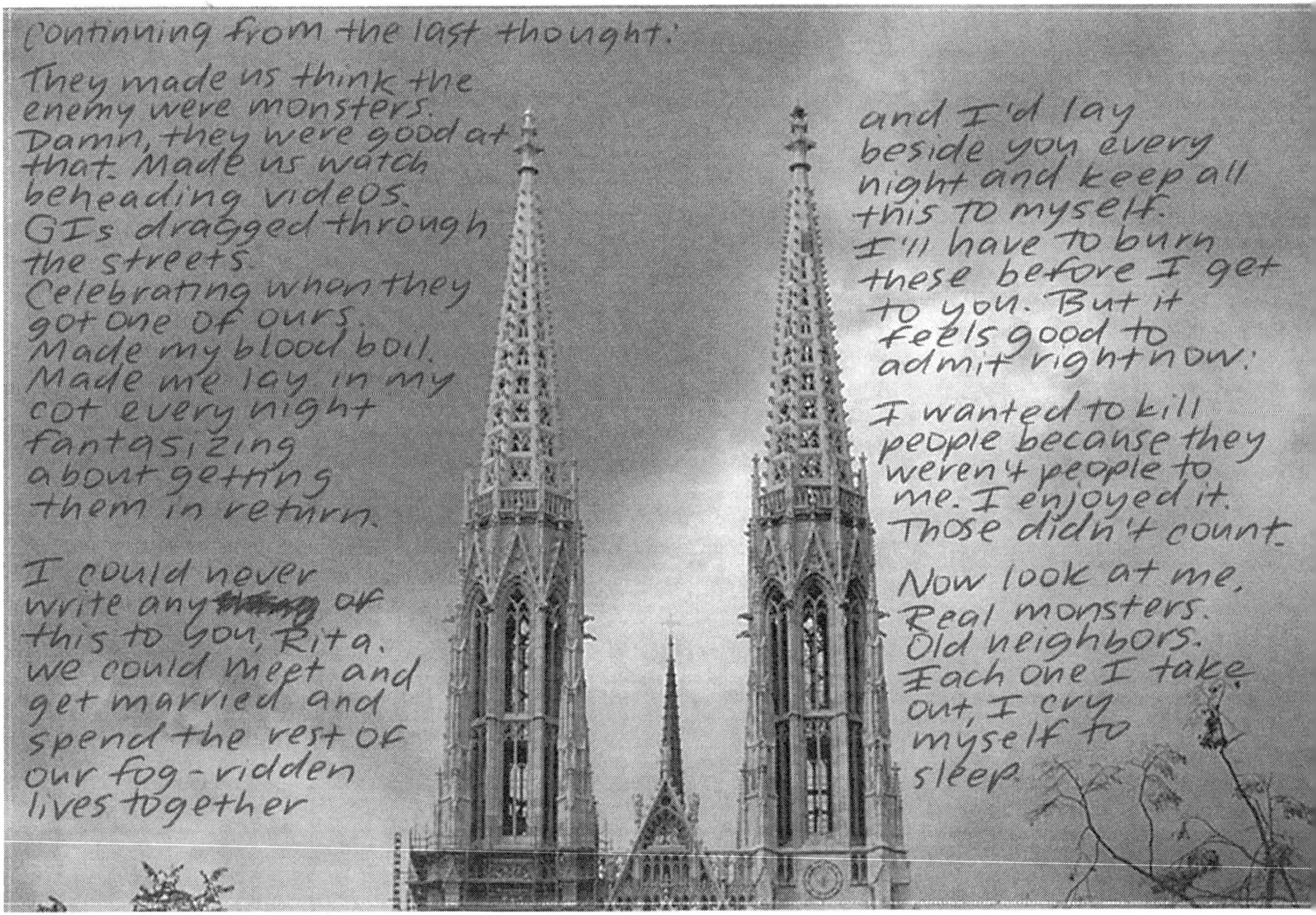

Continuing from the last thought:

They made us think the enemy were monsters. Damn, they were good at that. Made us watch beheading videos. GIs dragged through the streets. Celebrating when they got one of ours. Made my blood boil. Made me lay in my cot every night fantasizing about getting them in return.

I could never write any~~thing~~ of this to you, Rita. We could meet and get married and spend the rest of our fog-ridden lives together and I'd lay beside you every night and keep all this to myself. I'll have to burn these before I get to you. But it feels good to admit right now:

I wanted to kill people because they weren't people to me. I enjoyed it. Those didn't count.

Now look at me. Real monsters. Old neighbors. Each one I take out, I cry myself to sleep.

Where were you when it happened? What were you doing? Personally, I was underwater, scrubbing shit off the bottom of rich peoples' yachts. They're dead now, of course, and here I am, writing postcards while I wait for my pasta to cook, my arrabbiata sauce to warm through. Funny how the tide turns.

Man, I used to love diving, before it became my job. Then I hated it. Then it saved my life. Who the hell would've guessed?

All their money couldn't help them. Only oxygen. And I had plenty of that.

Rita

PLACE STAMP HERE

TO:

Time to admit that I'm only staying here because of the helium. Sent out the last of the balloons today and suddenly my side feels better. Our minds have too much power over us. A sixth thing I wish I'd learned earlier.

When the fog pulls back to the west, which I'm forecasting it will (the damn thing moves like it's alive, like it has a plan), I'm pushing toward the shopping mall just north of me. I always thought they were suicide, the big shopping centers that make for such alluring targots, but maybe I was wrong. Maybe enough time has passed.

Two big jugs of lemon-lime gatorade and every Zero bar I can fit in my pack. Down to 62 rounds of ammo. All those wasted years, eating nothing but Snickers.

I'm coming, Rita.

Hold tight.

To ???

I saw your balloon this morning. It floated in from the south. I fell over my own feet getting to the telescope in time to confirm what my instincts told me, and, sure enough, IT WASN'T ONE OF MINE.

PLACE STAMP HERE

There was a message attached, (same tactic I use). To grab it, though, would've meant going outside the building, leaving my safe haven, and I'm not ready for that yet. Will I ever be ready?

Who are you?

Where are you?

Why am I suddenly filled with a sense of dread?

I shall wait until the wind direction changes before sending this reply, in the hope it's seen. But that doesn't mean I'm ready to be found.

Rita

TO:

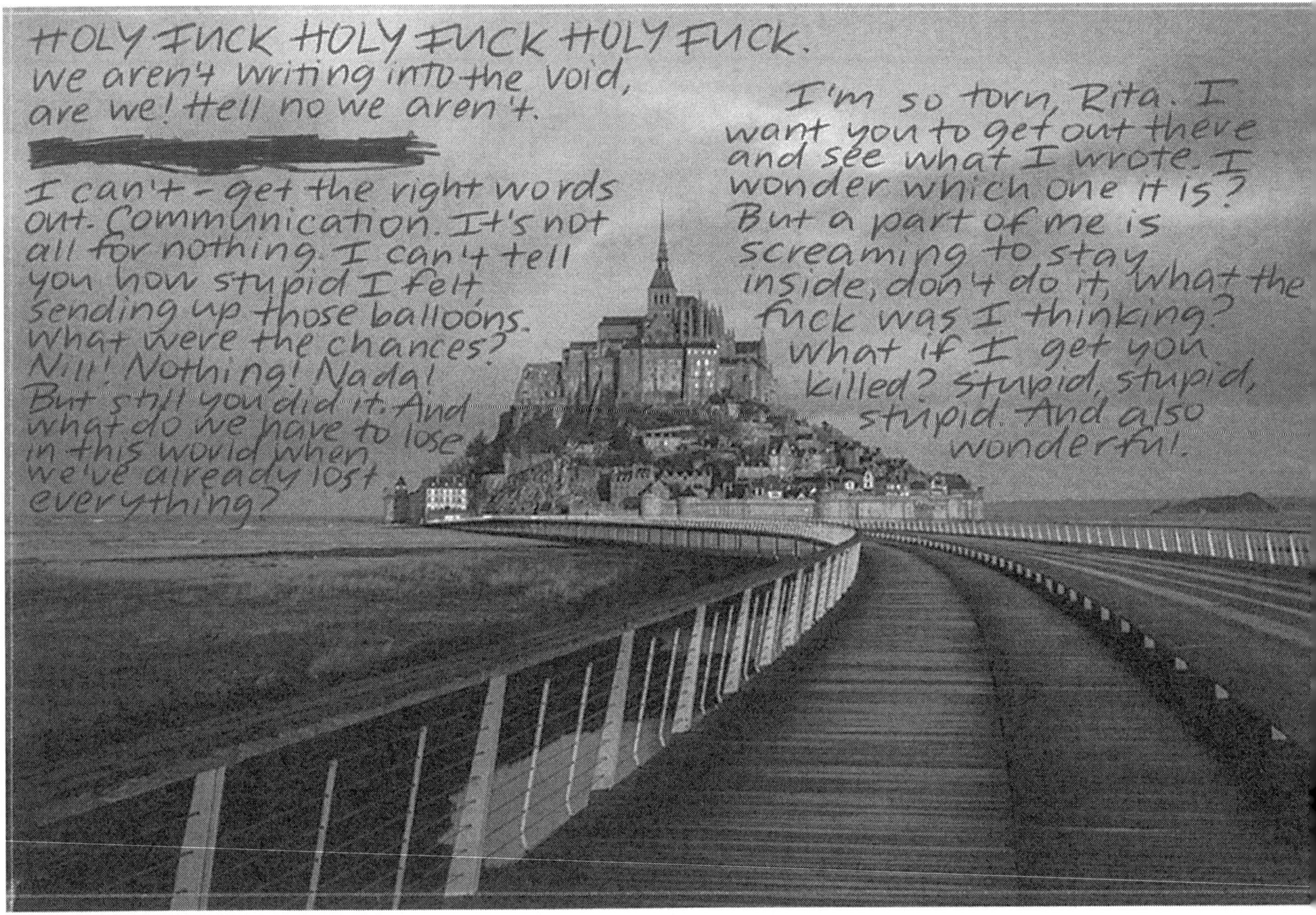

HOLY FUCK HOLY FUCK HOLY FUCK.
we aren't writing into the void,
are we! Hell no we aren't.
[redacted]
I can't - get the right words
out. Communication. It's not
all for nothing. I can't tell
you how stupid I felt
sending up those balloons.
What were the chances?
Nil! Nothing! Nada!
But still you did it. And
what do we have to lose
in this world when
we've already lost
everything?

I'm so torn, Rita. I
want you to get out there
and see what I wrote. I
wonder which one it is?
But a part of me is
screaming to stay
inside, don't do it, what the
fuck was I thinking?
What if I get you
killed? Stupid, stupid,
stupid. And also
wonderful.

Dear Stranger,

When I arrived here I was a dead person walking, with a day, maybe two, left in me. If I'd laid down to sleep, chances were I'd never have woken up. I was done. Then, from nowhere, this place appeared like a shimmering oasis, offering safety, supplies, somewhere to rest and heal. More than that, it became a home.

I never imagine myself leaving. To leave would be the greatest risk, and for what? The outside has nothing I need.

And yet –

All it took was a child's balloon for me to picture my life with someone else in it. Now I fantasize about a warm body next to mine at night, of the comfort that would bring. I dream about coming to find you.

But, no. I'm sorry. The fear is just too much.

Rita

PLACE STAMP HERE

TO:

I went outside. Only as far as the curb, where the entrance pavement meets the drop-off point, but I cannot tell you how hard my heart was pounding. I watched the trees the whole time.

Ground level = vulnerable.

I was out there mere seconds before running back inside, barricading the doors as I have done since the start. To quell my anxiety, I added extra boxes of rice and tins to the stack for good measure.

I keep thinking about what Mike used to say about burglars: 'If they want to get in, they'll get in'.

I spend most of my time in the staffroom now. Feels safer. Probably isn't.

Rita

PLACE STAMP HERE

TO:

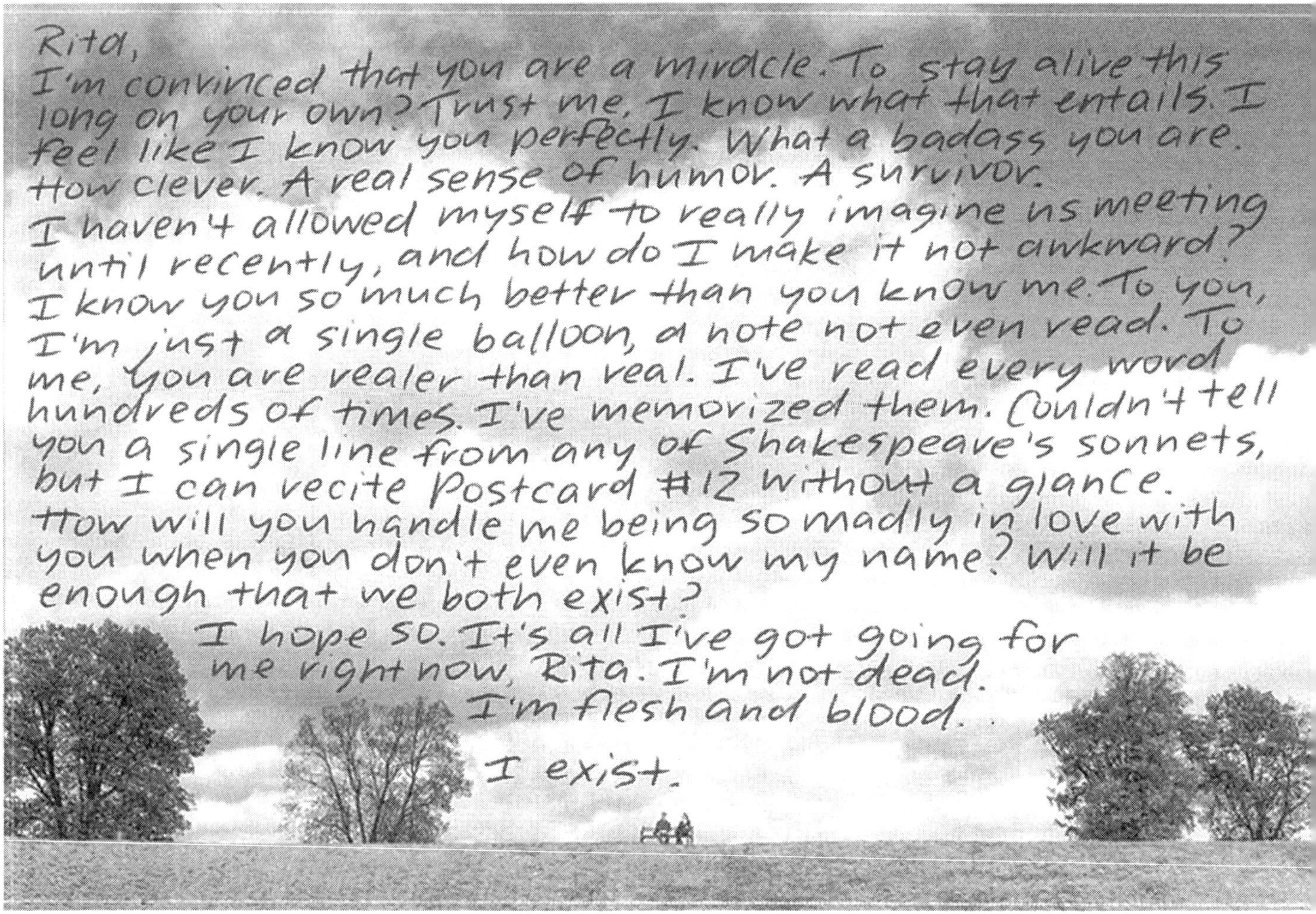

Rita,

I'm convinced that you are a miracle. To stay alive this long on your own? Trust me, I know what that entails. I feel like I know you perfectly. What a badass you are. How clever. A real sense of humor. A survivor.

I haven't allowed myself to really imagine us meeting until recently, and how do I make it not awkward? I know you so much better than you know me. To you, I'm just a single balloon, a note not even read. To me, you are realer than real. I've read every word hundreds of times. I've memorized them. Couldn't tell you a single line from any of Shakespeare's sonnets, but I can recite Postcard #12 without a glance. How will you handle me being so madly in love with you when you don't even know my name? Will it be enough that we both exist?

I hope so. It's all I've got going for me right now, Rita. I'm not dead. I'm flesh and blood.

I exist.

Life goes on. It escalates.
First, the insects returned, proliferating within weeks. No doubt due to the lack of competition, a shift in their ranking up the hierarchy, and the obscene amount of rotting matter to be had.
Then there was a resurgence in small, fast breeding mammals some months later. I assume their forebears survived somehow, safe and warm, in air pocket burrows deep underground. God bless hibernation.
Now, as I close my eyes, I'm lulled by the far-off, haunting call of an owl. I need it to be real.
Though I know firsthand how it feels to want something enough that you manifest it,
if only in your own mind.

Rita

PLACE
STAMP
HERE

TO:

Rita,

Plot twist: You don't exist, and I've been sending up both sets of balloons. How funny would that be?! I swear I started finding your notes right when I was about to give up. I was too scared to keep moving, running low on rations, seeing my ribs in mirrors. I do think we manifest our thoughts. I'm trying to keep them positive. Found four postcards in a single day today, can tell by the splurge that I'm zeroing in. Wasn't the mall — and best to forget the scenes of horror I found there - but I'm close. I'm patient.

I know what I want, and I think about it every day. Making it real. Making it real.

- Clayton

Mike.

s that you?

Don't be ridiculous, Rita. Of course it isn't. The dead don't write postcards. Whoever heard of such a thing?

All the same –

There's one caught on the rear wiper of a car parked out front.
A sorry looking balloon sags off it via a length of ribbon.
I can't bring myself to walk out that far, so instead I've aimed my telescope toward it, zoomed in as far as it goes.
I can see the image on the card clear as day: Disneyland.
So you understand, Mike, why I'm asking.
You always promised we'd go.

Rita

PLACE
STAMP
HERE

TO:

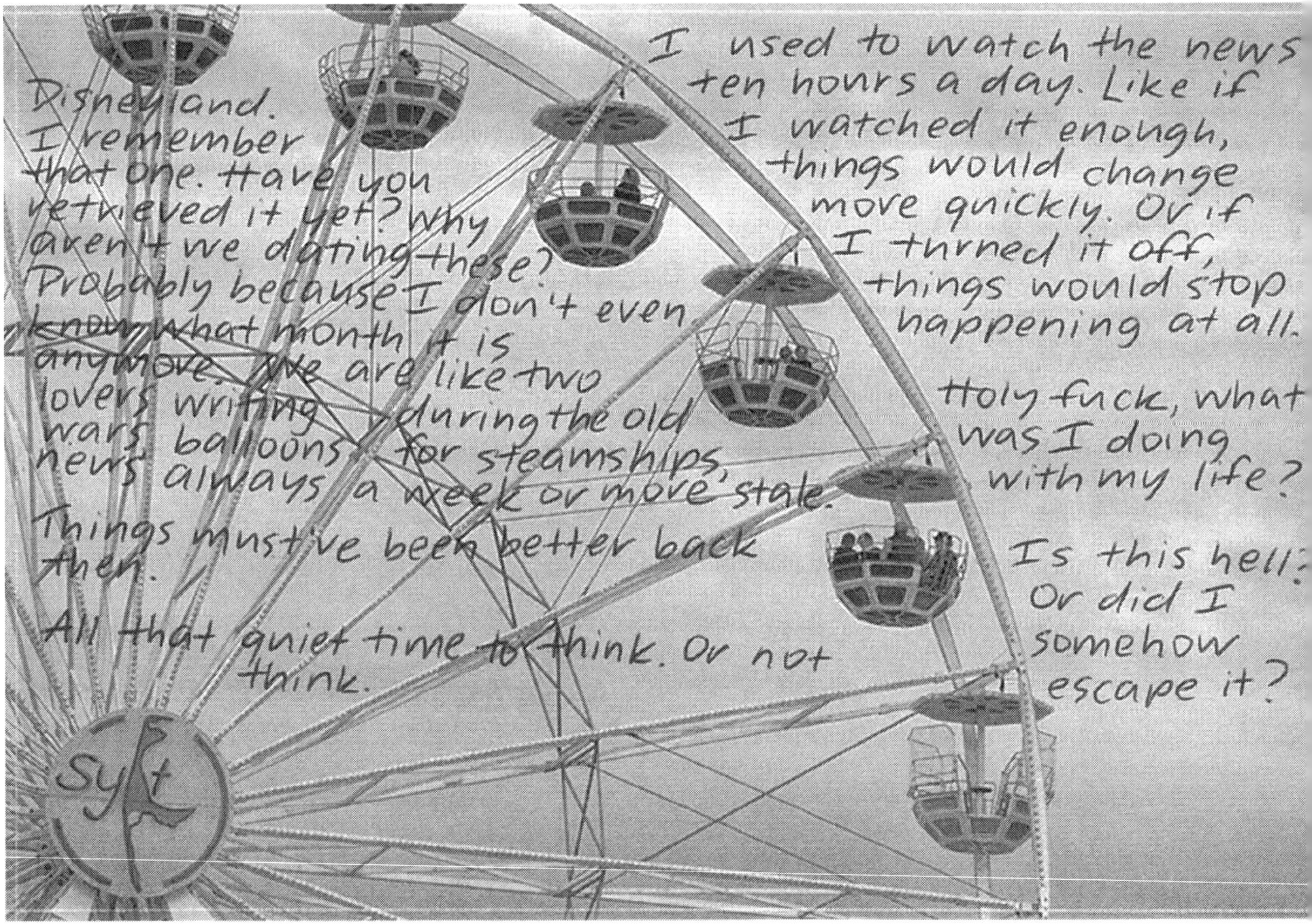

Disneyland.
I remember
that one. Have you
retrieved it yet? Why
aren't we dating these?
Probably because I don't even
know what month it is
anymore. We are like two
lovers writing during the old
wars, balloons for steamships,
news always a week or more stale.

Things must've been better back
then.

All that quiet time to think. Or not
think.

I used to watch the news
ten hours a day. Like if
I watched it enough,
things would change
move quickly. Or if
I turned it off,
things would stop
happening at all.

Holy fuck, what
was I doing
with my life?

Is this hell?
Or did I
somehow
escape it?

Wesley (my brother) and I were beach babies. We spent our summers outside of the usual parental limits, neck-deep and fearless, or jumping breakers in the surf. Rules were for city folk, not us.

There are so many things to miss, now, but the thing I miss most is the ocean. The smell of it, the freedom, the sense of possibility.

I've dragged a kayak onto the roof and am sitting on it. When I slow my breathing, there's sand on my shins, saltwater in my hair, which is drying into crisp curls in the sun. The rolling water undulates beneath me. I feel it. Muscle memory. Calm. I'm far from the land where sometimes I fear I will suffocate. I may stay and drift a while.

Rita

PLACE
STAMP
HERE

TO:

Rita,

Another confession that I will burn before I reach you:
When you say "beach," I imagine you in a bikini.
When you talk about water undulating,
you're in my arms. I'm close enough now that
I can't help but think about us touching. I
thought I was over any need for human
contact, but it's boiling up inside me now in a way
that frankly scares me.
In my dreams, we meet and just ravish each other.
Even though I know that's not how it can go.

Just in case, I started shaving again. Never
thought I'd lose that beard, Need to get some
sun on my face before I find you. Fuck me
and my thoughts.

-C

Dear Mike,

I still don't know who sent the Disneyland postcard.
I'm working to beat my agoraphobia, and am currently reading about self-hypnosis. Can't hurt, right?
Twice this week I went outside. Each time I made it slightly further from the door. My hands shook so much I was terrified the gun would go off, letting whatever, or whoever, took the bodies of Tomasz and his pals know I was there.
Did I mention I found a gun? Yeah, I'm a badass.
I'll try to get further. I need to know it's not you, if only for the sake of my sanity.

Rita

PLACE
STAMP
HERE

TO:

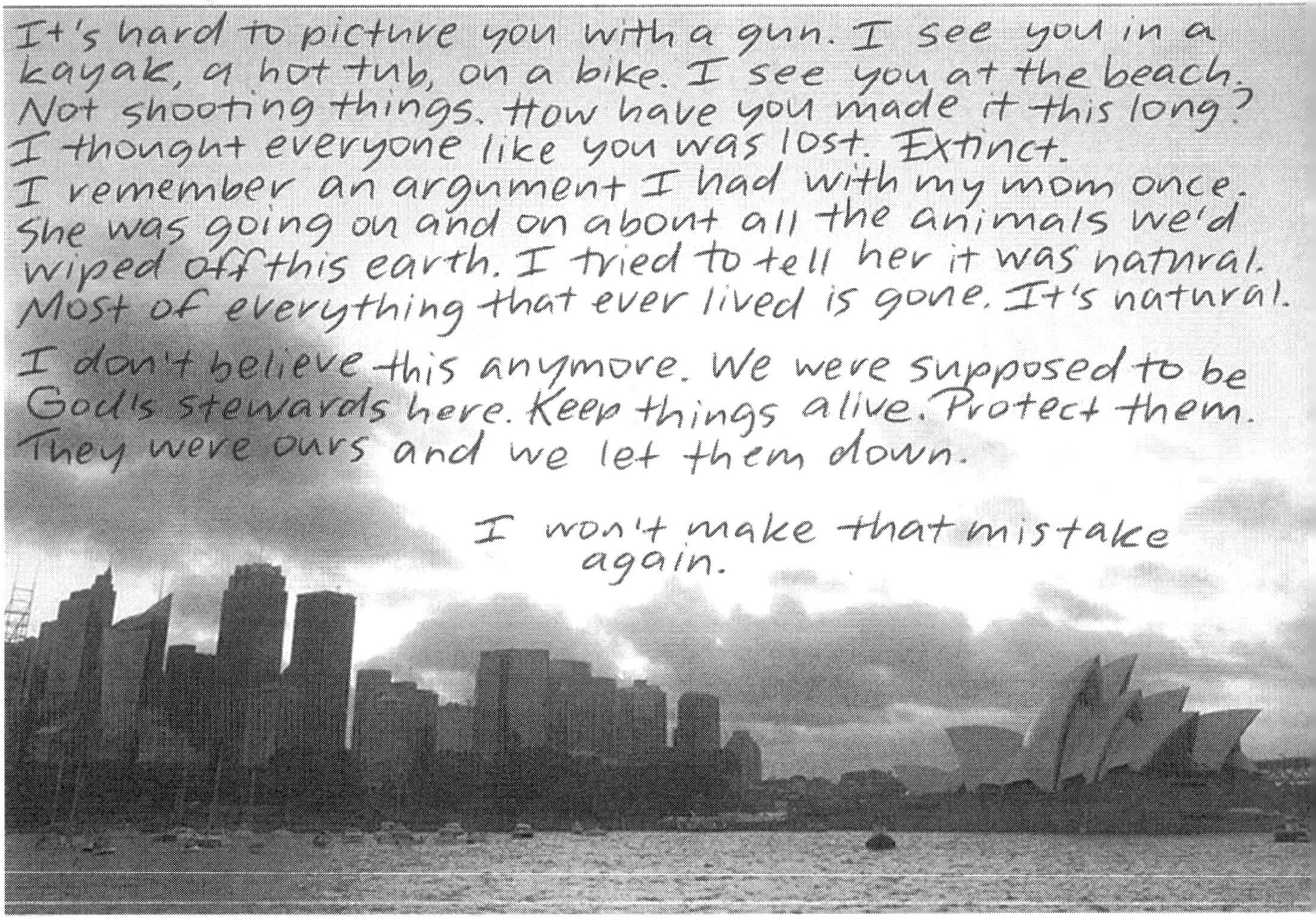
It's hard to picture you with a gun. I see you in a kayak, a hot tub, on a bike. I see you at the beach. Not shooting things. How have you made it this long? I thought everyone like you was lost. Extinct.
I remember an argument I had with my mom once. She was going on and on about all the animals we'd wiped off this earth. I tried to tell her it was natural. Most of everything that ever lived is gone. It's natural.
I don't believe this anymore. We were supposed to be God's stewards here. Keep things alive. Protect them. They were ours and we let them down.
I won't make that mistake again.

was woken early by a loud noise. I first thought of gunfire, but that's crazy, right? I haven't seen a living erson in forever. Not since –

Yes, well, best we don't mention the fairground.

My next thought was a car backfiring, which is even crazier, given there isn't a working car engine for miles around. I should know. I tried most of them on my way here, to no avail.

Nothing in the store appeared to have been disturbed, and believe me I checked, so I went to the roof, stared out as far as I could in the shitty gray visibility. Listening. Listening...

To nothing. Not even a sparrow.

guess the latest development is that I'm hearing things now.

Fan-freakin-tastic.

Rita

PLACE
STAMP
HERE

TO:

My Rita,

Funny, that's how I think of you: my Rita.

~~Confe~~ Confession time — I have a lot to confess. Mike's dead. You know it, I know it. And I can't hide the fact I'm happy about that. Because if he wasn't dead, I don't know what I'd do.

Another lie. I know exactly what I'd do, and old Mikey-boy wouldn't like it too much. Because I'd fight for you, Rita. Which is a polite way of saying I'd kick the living shit out of that asshole you call a husband.

Unsurprisingly, this won't be going up on a balloon, because this card is, like you, only for me.

My miracle.

My Rita.

Motherfucker:

I made it to the car. And the Disneyland postcard. As I tried to untangle one from the other a panic hit me like I've never known, so I ran, tearing the card from its mooring in the process.

In what was not my finest moment, I fell up the curb, twisting my ankle good, and only just managed to hop inside. Damn clumsy idiot. If it's broken, I'm screwed.

At least now I know my dead husband isn't writing to me from under a cold pile of rocks. No. Instead it's someone else. Someone with the most wonderful name I've ever heard. Wherefore art thou, Clayton?

Rita

PLACE STAMP HERE

TO:

Top five excuses for sobbing like a child, screaming into the void, and crying some more:

1) Holy fuck it worked. Sent a thought into the clouds, and it found you. Just like you found me.
2) The relief that you got back inside. Please, please, please no more risks like that. I'm not sending another note. Can't put you in danger. Can't.
3) That ankle. Please be a sprain. We take the little injuries for granted, but those are the ones that get us in the end.
4) You wrote my name.
   I've stared at it for God knows how long today, trying to imagine it from your lips. Our names are weird, aren't they? When we hear them. When we see them. The most familiar thing in the world, but it hits like electricity.
5) The most wonderful name you've ever heard? No words for how that makes me feel.

I'm a mess right now, Rita. Hold tight. You'll be in my arms soon.

For the record, three bits of shitty news:

1. My BMX career might be over. With an ankle the size of a grapefruit, I can barely walk. Stairs are also an issue, so I'm back sleeping in the shed on the shop floor (shitty enough news by itself).
2. The gun is gone. I dropped it outside when I fell, was just about building up the courage to retrieve it, but when I looked this morning it was no longer there.
3. I'm down to my last cylinder of helium.

As Ritadays go, I've had better.

Rita

PLACE STAMP HERE

TO:

____

____

____

Are you a God-fearing woman, Rita? I was a believer my whole life, more or less, until the world got fucked up. Even then [redacted] a part of me asked if the annihilation wasn't just our Lord's way of taking care of business.

With hindsight, I can't see the sense in it. Why would God want me to kill children? The one in the fog. The others. How does that fit His plan?

I have to live with all I've done, the confused look on those kid's faces, forever and ever, amen. Is that my punishment? What kind of unmerciful bastard God does that to a man?

But then I remember you. My heart soars. I wonder what I did to deserve finding you out there in our mutual urban wilderness.

I find myself believing in something again.

Are you my salvation?

PLACE
STAMP
HERE

Dear Wes,

Your medical skills must've rubbed off! I had an accident, broke my ankle, I think. Stupid of me, really, given the state of things. But, there you go. You never told me it hurt so much when you fell off the bridge that time. Or maybe you did, and I ignored you. I vaguely remember making fun of you (I had no idea!) so for that I'm truly sorry.

It wasn't getting better (can you die from a broken ankle?) but luckily there's a ton of stuff around here. I made a cast using cotton wadding and strips of t-shirts dipped in plaster of Paris, and a crutch from a broom.

Guess we're both doctors now, huh?

Rita

TO:

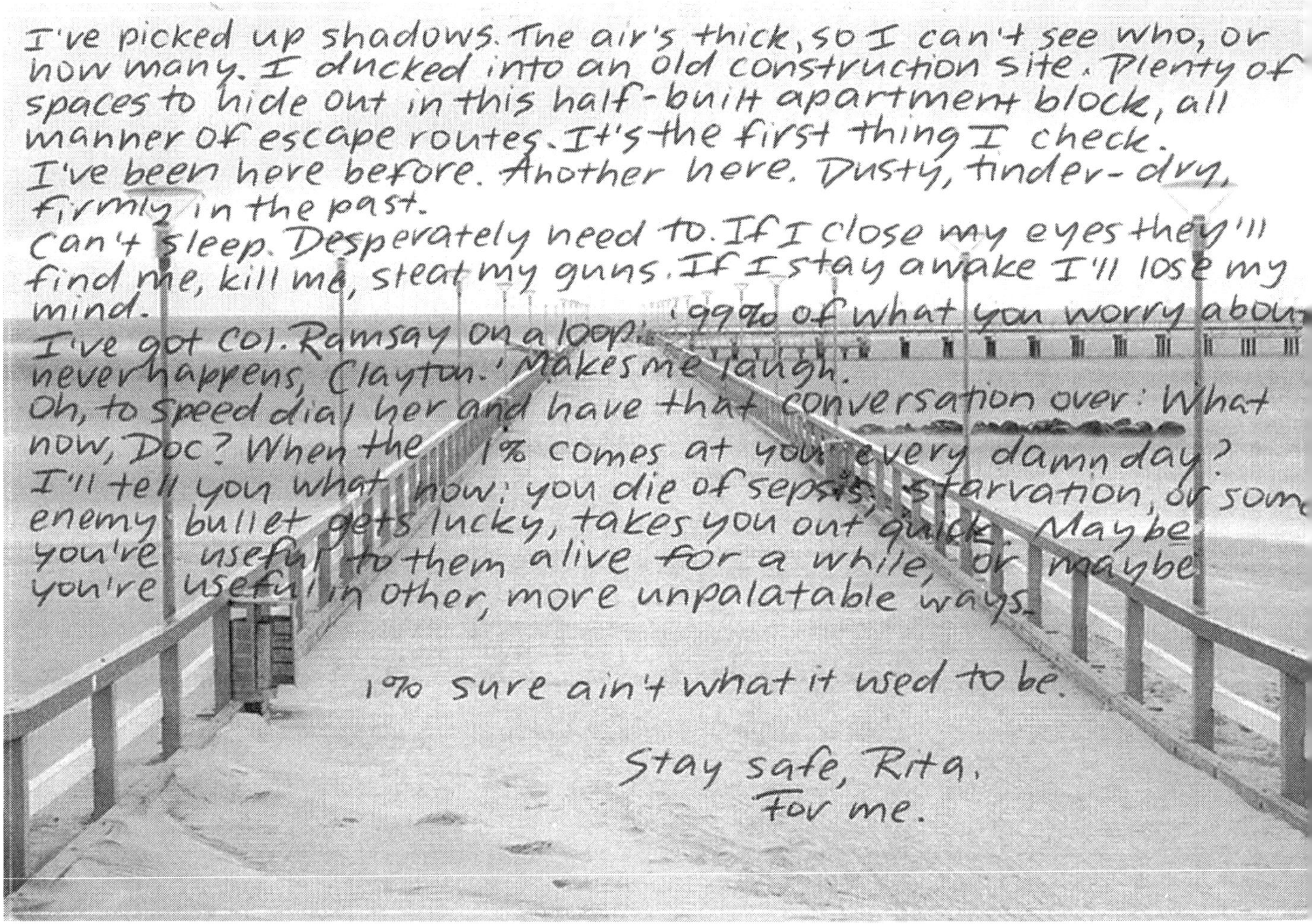

I've picked up shadows. The air's thick, so I can't see who, or how many. I ducked into an old construction site. Plenty of spaces to hide out in this half-built apartment block, all manner of escape routes. It's the first thing I check.
I've been here before. Another here. Dusty, tinder-dry, firmly in the past.
Can't sleep. Desperately need to. If I close my eyes they'll find me, kill me, steal my guns. If I stay awake I'll lose my mind.
I've got Col. Ramsay on a loop: '99% of what you worry about never happens, Clayton.' Makes me laugh.
Oh, to speed dial her and have that conversation over: What now, Doc? When the 1% comes at you every damn day?
I'll tell you what now: you die of sepsis, starvation, or some enemy bullet gets lucky, takes you out quick. Maybe you're useful to them alive for a while, or maybe you're useful in other, more unpalatable ways.

1% sure ain't what it used to be.

Stay safe, Rita.
For me.

ear Clayton,

orry it's taken me this long to reply.

could say I was unwell, or that I hid your words away,
onvinced myself you weren't real, or that the breeze
lew north instead of south. And while all those things
re true, they aren't the reason.

he reason is life was easier that way, you know? Without you.
f you are real then I have decisions to make, choices, options,
nd I haven't had those for such a long time. Accepting you're
ut there takes a sledgehammer to the walls I've built around
nyself. I'm still not sure that's wise.

orgive me. I need more time to think.

Rita

PLACE
STAMP
HERE

TO:

____

____

____

seeing my name, imagining you saying it, is the closest thing to sex I've had in years. My body reacts. The lack of control terrifies and thrills me in equal measure. Wanting it to stop, but needing it more than anything. You have no idea.

Five balloons – there's that number again – five balloons went by today. My guts twist when I think of what you might have said on those postcards. What I missed out on. The intimacy lost.

Too many damn ferals camped between here and wherever you are for me to shoot your messages down. I hear them hunting at dusk (I'd like to say for rats, but I suspect they go for distinctly larger prey these days).

From what I hear there are at least a dozen. I like my chances against a handful, I'm a good enough shot to take down four, maybe six, before they even know I'm there, but not twelve. So I'll bide my time, maybe pick off stragglers with my knife.

That's one thing the fog is good for.

Seems I lost a number of days to my new best friends: a fine single malt whiskey, and painkillers scavenged from a dead man. Which, depending on how you look at it, either don't go well together, or go together a bit too well.

This was all peachy until last night, when I received a surprise visit from my father. The same father we buried in '08.

'Little pig, little pig,' he said, tapping on the door to my shed. 'Let me in.' (I had the presence of mind to lock myself in, at least).

Way to sober me up, Dad.

Needless to say, I'm sleeping back in the staff room from now on. Stairs or no stairs.

Rita

PLACE STAMP HERE

TO:

Want to know what my dad would say if he could see me now? 'Man up, Clayton'.

No, that's not quite it.

He'd say: 'Man the fuck up, Clayton'. With a smack of the head to make damn sure I got the message through my thick skull.

And I'd be grateful for the reminder. Sure as shit wouldn't have lived this long if not for him, raising me right, making me strong.

I've cried more tears these last few weeks than in my whole life. Going soft. Dad wouldn't approve. But then, he never did.

Tomorrow I'm pushing on. Manning up.

Save some of that sweet-sounding whiskey for yours truly.

Governor,

For a long while I thought it was about intellectual property, that you had some vested interest in the project, in the tech, in the outcome, financial or otherwise. Why else would you rush the launch through?

Did you know it would go this badly wrong? Was that the plan from the start?

How you must've laughed when you promised us a solution, and we bought it without question. We gobbled your gold-plated savior bullshit right up.

So, what now, hero? How long until the atmosphere clears? Do you know, or even care?

Rita

PLACE STAMP HERE

TO:

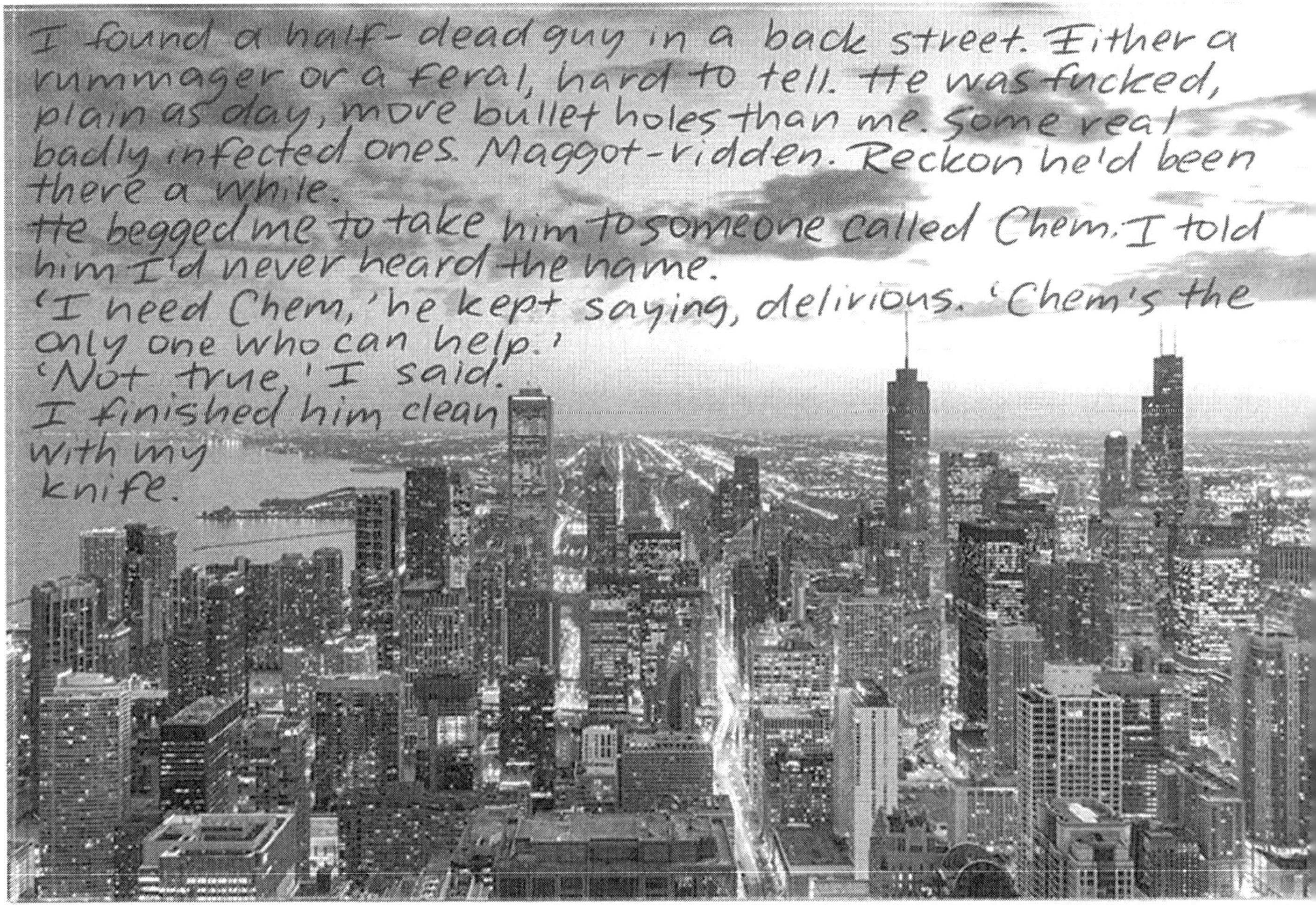

I found a half-dead guy in a back street. Either a rummager or a feral, hard to tell. He was fucked, plain as day, more bullet holes than me. Some real badly infected ones. Maggot-ridden. Reckon he'd been there a while.

He begged me to take him to someone called Chem. I told him I'd never heard the name.

'I need Chem,' he kept saying, delirious. 'Chem's the only one who can help.'

'Not true,' I said.

I finished him clean
with my
knife.

figured a building inspection was overdue so hopped around using a pair of brooms. I wish I hadn't as another breach has appeared, this time down the cookware aisle. No kidding, it's the size of a fucking bear.

While I enjoyed my short pain holiday, courtesy of Percocet Airways, something tore out a full panel from the warehouse wall, and clawed through the brick, into the main building.

What could do that? And how did I not hear it?

Then again, maybe I did. (Little pig, little pig...)

Must do an inventory to check if anything is missing, food-wise. I don't feel safe here anymore, but where the hell else is there to go?

Rita

PLACE
STAMP
HERE

TO:

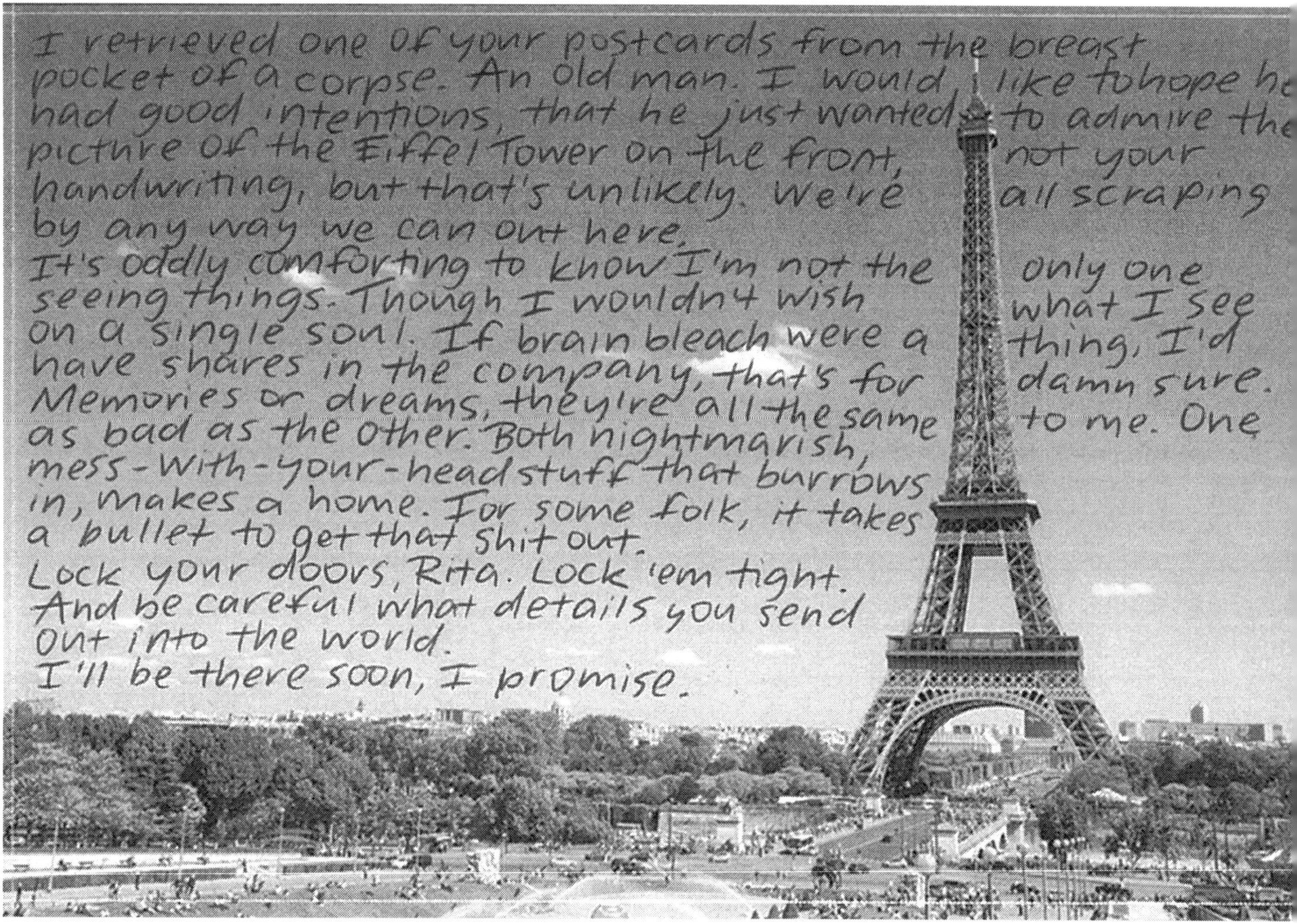

I retrieved one of your postcards from the breast pocket of a corpse. An old man. I would like to hope he had good intentions, that he just wanted to admire the picture of the Eiffel Tower on the front, not your handwriting, but that's unlikely. We're all scraping by any way we can out here.
It's oddly comforting to know I'm not the only one seeing things. Though I wouldn't wish what I see on a single soul. If brain bleach were a thing, I'd have shares in the company, that's for damn sure. Memories or dreams, they're all the same to me. One as bad as the other. Both nightmarish, mess-with-your-head stuff that burrows in, makes a home. For some folk, it takes a bullet to get that shit out.
Lock your doors, Rita. Lock 'em tight. And be careful what details you send out into the world.
I'll be there soon, I promise.

Dear Clayton,
I watch from morning 'til night for your messages.
On fog-free days I lie on the window ledge, wrapped in a blanket. I eat tinned pears and scour the landscape for balloons from beyond the southern hills.
I've spotted two more so far, since the first one, but they were out of reach. (I'm injured; did I mention that?) It damn near kills me to sit here helplessly as they float by.
I wonder what you wrote. I wonder who you wrote it for.
And deep down I hope that person is me.

Rita

PLACE STAMP HERE

TO:

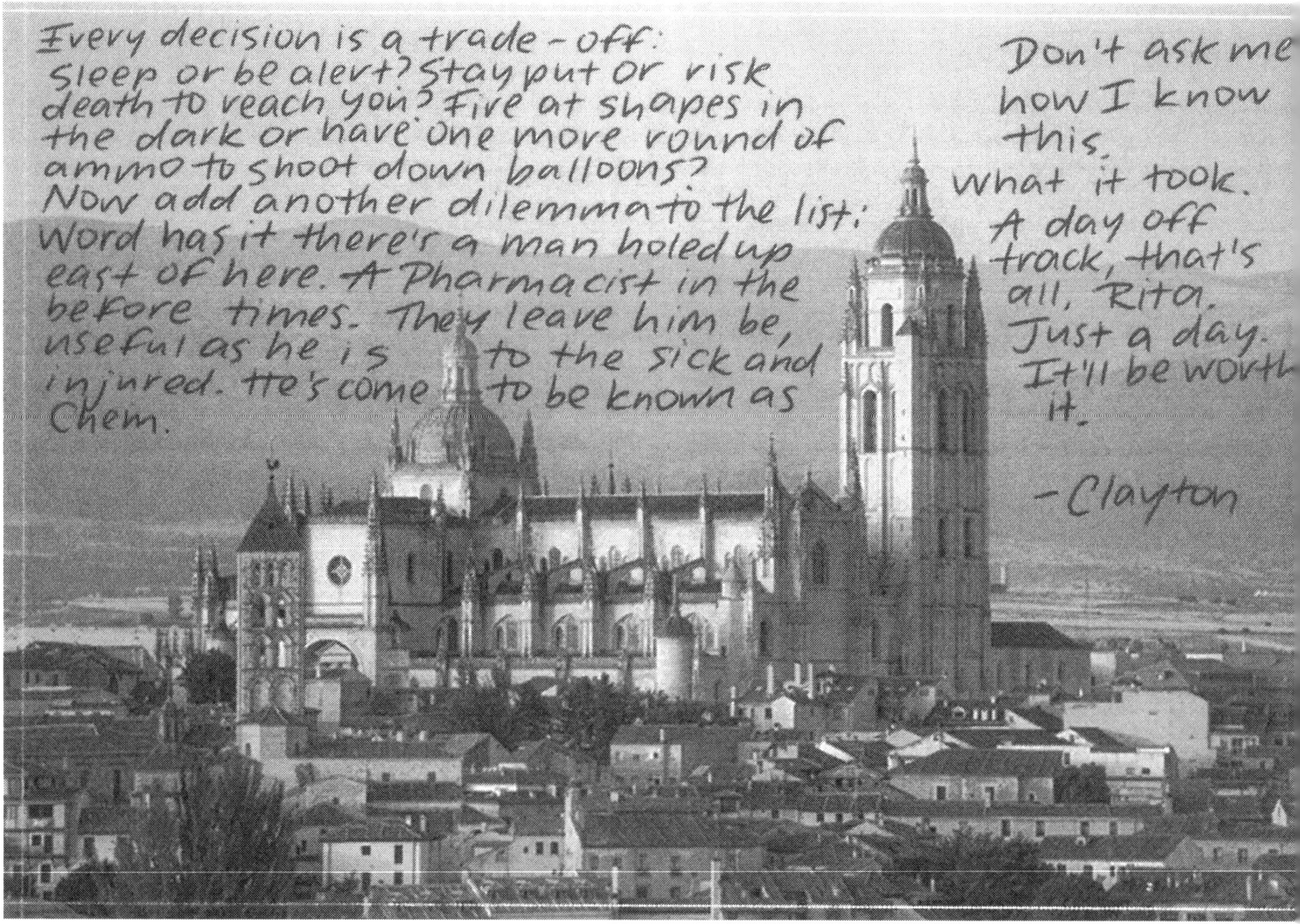

Every decision is a trade-off:
sleep or be alert? Stay put or risk
death to reach you? Fire at shapes in
the dark or have one more round of
ammo to shoot down balloons?
Now add another dilemma to the list:
Word has it there's a man holed up
east of here. A Pharmacist in the
before times. They leave him be,
useful as he is to the sick and
injured. He's come to be known as
Chem.

Don't ask me
how I know
this.
What it took.
A day off
track, that's
all, Rita.
Just a day.
It'll be worth
it.

—Clayton

:layton,

lere's the thing: I'm battling some serious trust
ssues right now.

trusted my husband, Mike, when he suddenly had
ll those 'after-work events' to attend. I trusted
hat Gov. Merck was trying to save all our futures, not
ust his own. I trusted the walls of this place to protect me
rom whatever is out there in the fog, trying to get in.
Trust is finite, and, frankly, I'm all out.

So –

:an I trust you, Clayton? That's the big question. Because
'm starting to think nothing is what it seems.

Rita

PLACE
STAMP
HERE

TO:

So much for one day. Did I really expect to waltz in there and have them hand everything over? Dumbass.
Thank Christ for my emergency M&Ms stash. Three days hidden in a rusted out SUV. Those goddamn peanutty fuckers got me through. Suffice to say, I got the pills I needed. Just. I'm writing this from out back of a Walmart. I did wonder briefly if you were inside, but it's single story and ransacked, so no, not your place. Shame, I could do with a hot tub about now. There is, however, a tank of helium dumped near the trash. Hallelujah! I'll send my last few greeting cards off into the mist. I hope they find you.

-Clayton

PS. Yes, you can trust me. The things I've done for you.

I've set a trap. Fear got me nowhere, so I'm finding out who, or what, keeps breaking in at night, and I'm facing that bastard down. Nobody trashes my place and gets away with it.

After dinner, I built a half-assed barricade across the most recent hole in the wall. Not enough to stop someone getting in, just enough to look like I tried. Balanced on top is a basket of the noisiest things I could find: pans, cutlery, ornaments, jingle bells, anything to make one heck of a clang as it hits the floor. They're not getting in without me knowing about it.

And now to bed.

Rita

P.S. Fun fact: My leg cast makes the perfect holster for a carving knife.

PLACE STAMP HERE

TO:

There's a scar on my thigh. Mostly, I forget it's there. They said they got all the shrapnel out, even showed me the X-ray to prove it, when it kept playing up. Man, is it playing up now.

Certain things set it off. Actions or events that trigger memories of that day. The bad choices. The dull kick of steel piercing flesh in an instant.

Five statements of fact:

1) Chem wouldn't give up the drugs.
2) I can't fail another mission.
3) Shooting first was the only choice.
4) I didn't know Chem was a she.
5) No more headspace for regrets.

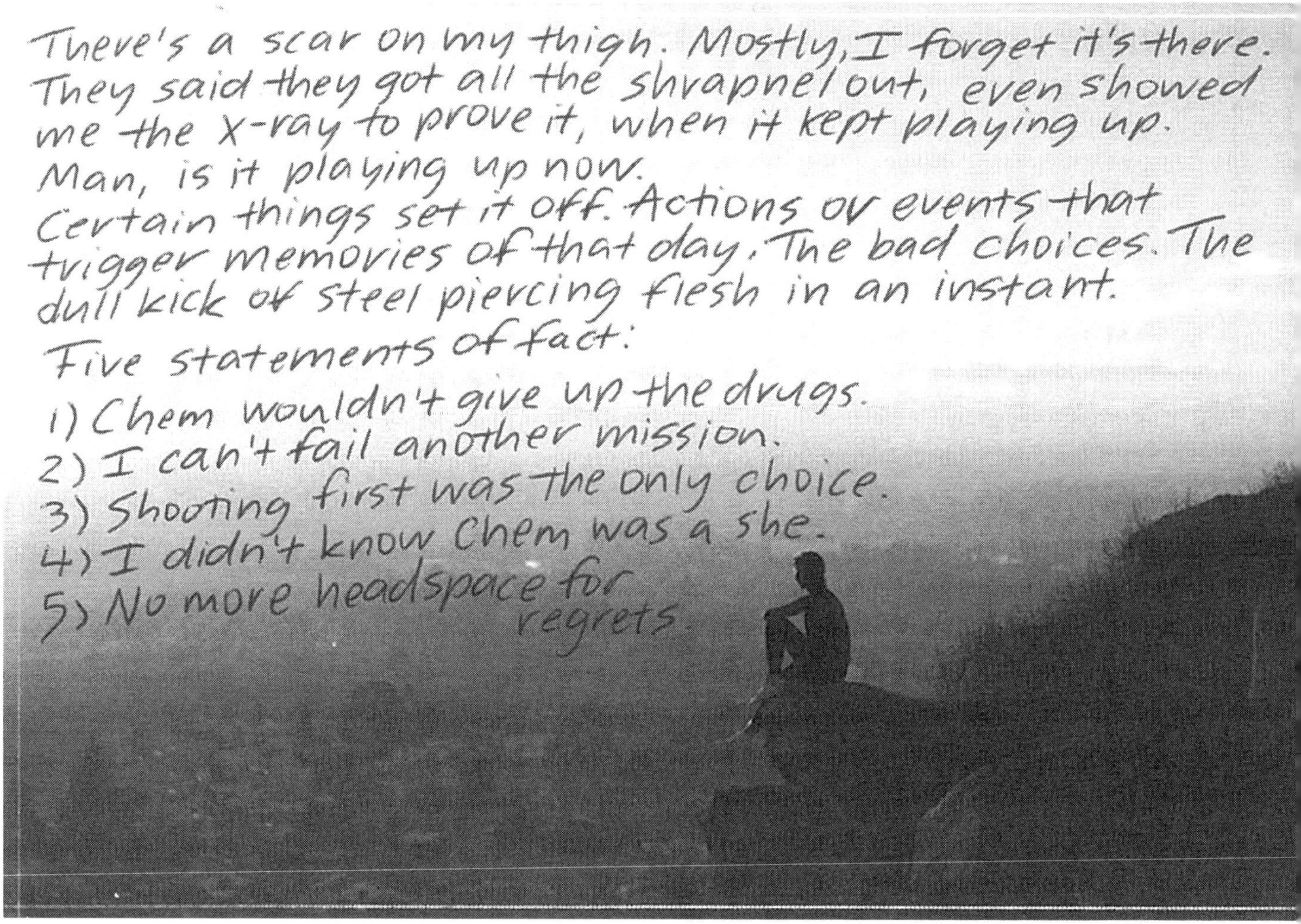

Do you believe in curses, Clayton? Are the dead paying the price for their misdeeds, do you think, or are we?

PLACE STAMP HERE

I have a confession: prior to the launch I wished for the kind of time and space I have now. Prayed for it. I pictured a world where nobody demanded anything of me, where Mike didn't exist, where I was free to pass the hours as I wanted.

It might sound strange but I wasn't unhappy, or lonely, before you came along. Really I wasn't. Sad for the world, of course, who wouldn't be? But never lonely, and never sad for myself.

Then, there you were.

You cursed me, Clayton.

I'm to be tormented by messages, close enough to see but never read.

Rita

TO:

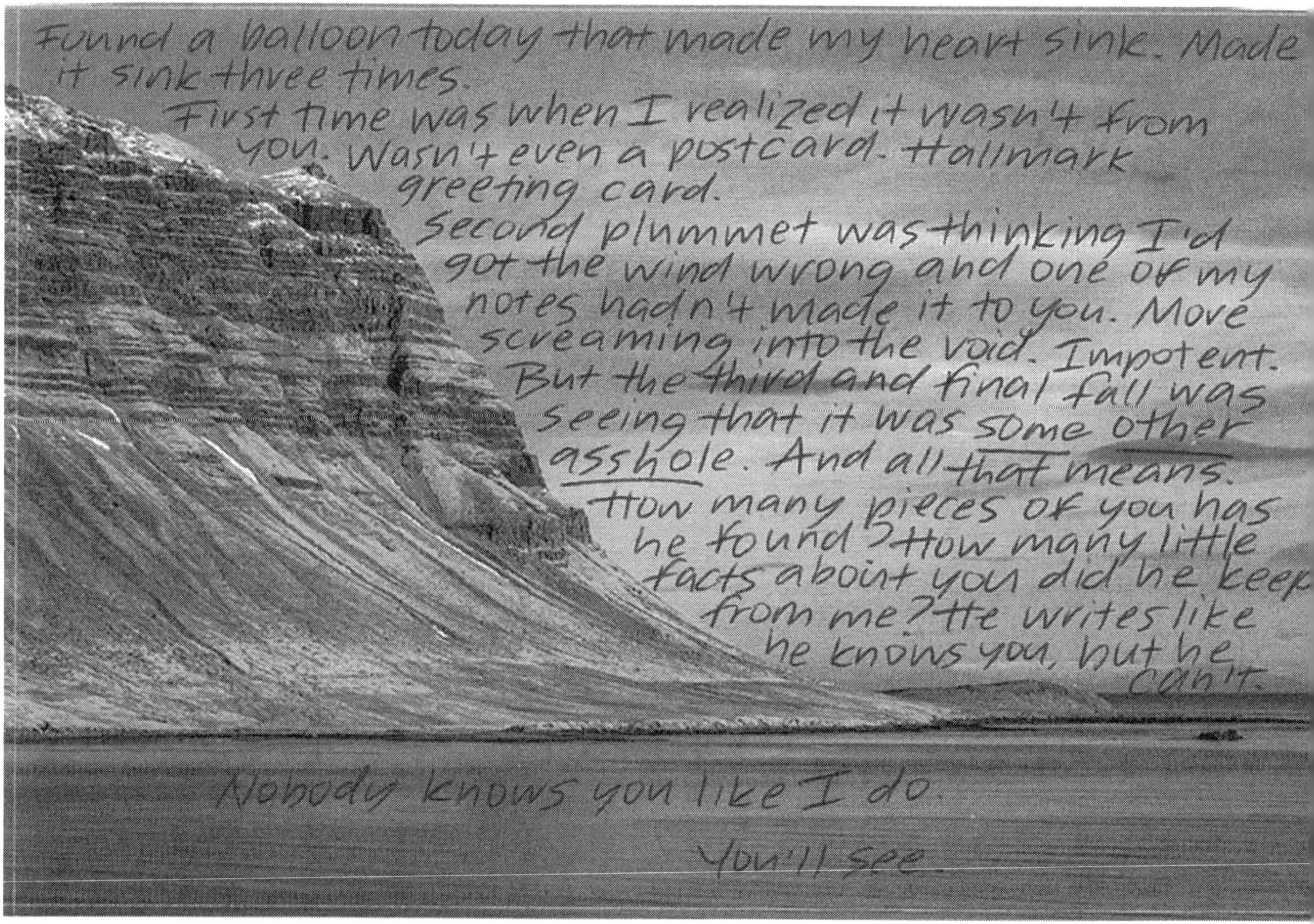

Found a balloon today that made my heart sink. Made it sink three times.

First time was when I realized it wasn't from you. Wasn't even a postcard. Hallmark greeting card.

Second plummet was thinking I'd got the wind wrong and one of my notes hadn't made it to you. More screaming into the void. Impotent.

But the third and final fall was seeing that it was some other asshole. And all that means.

How many pieces of you has he found? How many little facts about you did he keep from me? He writes like he knows you, but he can't.

Nobody knows you like I do.

You'll see.

The worst things to happen to me are as follows...

1. Mom's slide into dementia.
2. IVF (the drugs, the miscarriage, the whole shebang).
3. Dad leaving.
4. The high school years.
5. Mike.

Well, well, Apocalypse, not even top 5.
How disappointed you must be.

Rita

PLACE STAMP HERE

TO:

I get it now. Can't believe it took this long, but now I get it. What the therapy was for. Why the Army tears us down and how they make us want to die for some asshole we just met two months ago. Why my relationships never worked.

We're supposed to confess these things to each other, aren't we? Have that <u>one</u> person we trust to admit how much we're hurting. I hear you, Rita. I actually want to listen. I mean that. To every word. While you tell me about your mom, so we can both remember her. Tell me about how hard you tried in the past while we rock our baby to sleep. Tell me about Mike while I give you the man you've dreamed of.

I'll share my hurts with you. I get it now. It's what it's all about, isn't it?

ear Wes,

'm going to have to let you go, real soon. I must take ll the wonderful memories I have of you, and of us, and pack them away neatly before they turn sour. f there's one last thing I want to tell you before you go, it's that I was so proud to call you my brother. So damn proud.

You did good, kid.

Oh, and for the record, don't think I didn't notice you were Mom and Dad's favorite. But that's okay. You were my favorite too.

Love you always,
Rita Skeeter

PLACE STAMP HERE

TO:

The winds are fickle, aren't they? The fog has a mind of its own. I can feel it sometimes, the totality of it all, moving like a giant beast with beating organs and limbs like fat sausages of gas moving across the streets and hugging these buildings, and pushing me a block over from where I wanna be, and another block, this way and that, like life sometimes.

Probably shouldn't take these pills with beer. I'm the fog now. My brain at least. Saving the rest for you, my Rita. For your leg. Gotta watch infection. It spreads, you know?

We infected the world, didn't we? I used to throw garbage out the window. Earth was big. Plenty big enough for us. No way we could fuck this up. I don't feel any pain right now, and that feels good. Maybe lived most of my life this way.

Governor,

The stories I could tell you about my brother. I said goodbye to him today. Not in person, not face to face, my arms around him, as it should've been.

No. My goodbye was scratched onto a postcard of all things.

A fucking Costco postcard.

He was the last of them. The last person I cared about who I held out any shred of hope of not having perished in those first days.

But we know in our hearts the truth of it, you and I, don't we?

My baby brother is dead.

Rita

PLACE
STAMP
HERE

TO:

HOLY SHIT. I'm such an idiot. Of course. I went right past that Costco last week, didn't look like a place you could hole up in, or maybe thought the roof was wrong from how I pictured it, or I'm a chickenshit who knows that parking lot is a fucking killing zone.

Costco. Jesus H. Christ, Rita, you've gotta be more careful, letting shit slip like that. There are other people out here. They aren't all good men like me. I don't think they'd all want to take care of you the way I do.

Gotta push harder. The urgency now.

Gotta ~~shut you~~ teach you what not to say.

The fog comes in varying levels of opacity. At its most dense, you'd struggle to find your own rear end with both hands.

The middling fog, more of a mist than a true fog, renders even the mundane view of the car lot otherworldly. Quite beautiful. Visual range: fifty yards, at most.

Then there's this, a kind of heaviness. Even indoors you can feel it when you breathe. It's humidity and residue and fungal spores and rot. Not thick enough to have form, only presence. Not weather so much as mood.

I long for a breeze to clear the air.

Rita

PLACE STAMP HERE

TO:

Dear Clayton,

Just when I feared the ink would wear away from my constant rereading of your postcard, what should I spy through my telescope?

Yes! Yes! Another balloon! Another beguiling message! Caught up in the branch of a tree, a hundred yards or so away. Lord only knows when it landed. It took forever for the last fog to clear.

Although it's at the other end of the parking lot, way too far away for me to retrieve, know this: I shall savor the sight of it.

I'd all but given up.

Your friend,
Rita

PLACE STAMP HERE

TO:

Fuck, this is where the confusion sets in. How long ago did you send this? So many things could be true right now:

* I'm reading an old message of yours. It's possible. I've gotten pretty good at judging how long ink has been out in the weather, but this one was in a tree, off the ground.
* You're seeing an old message of mine that somehow stayed aloft these last four days? Unlikely. But maybe I know less about balloons than I thought? These last months, figured I was an expert.
* The order is all wrong. Everything I've collected to now. I know this, always have, but I tend to forget. I keep them in the order I found them, and I read them over and over that way.

* Don't want to think this one, but I guess I've already known it: other people are writing to you. I swear to God Rita, if I see their names in your handwriting, I don't know that my heart will make it.

Dear Clayton,

Last night I saw you in a dream. You lived in an identical store to mine, as far south from the hills as I am to their north.

In every way, we mirrored each other, each day doing the same things, following the same routines, neither of us moving from our respective, isolated lives.

Both of us died alone.

Is that how it's to be? Or will one of us risk everything for the other?

Thinking of you (us?).

Rita

P. S. Not feeling great. Will write more when I shake off this cold.

PLACE STAMP HERE

TO:

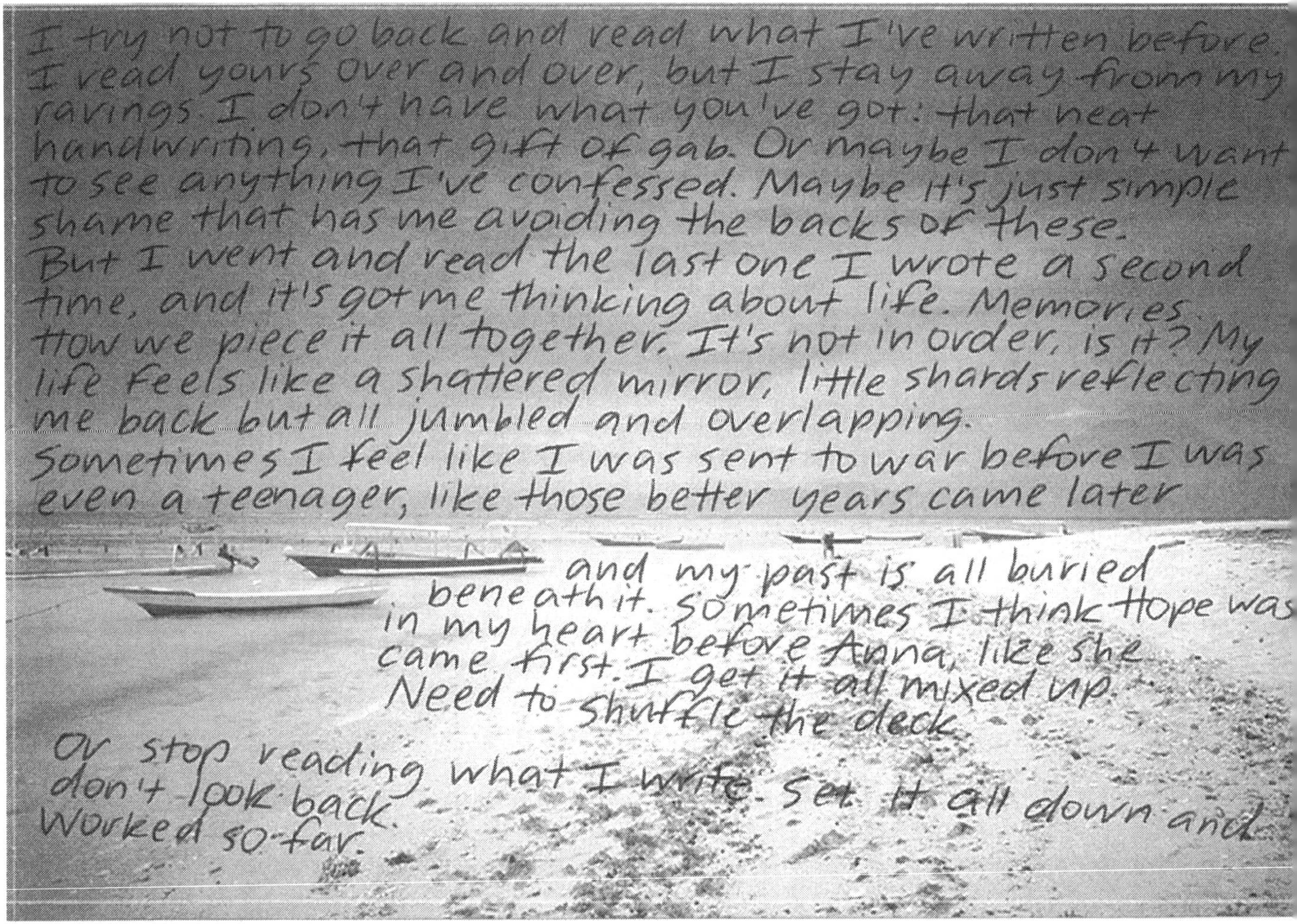

I try not to go back and read what I've written before. I read yours over and over, but I stay away from my ravings. I don't have what you've got: that neat handwriting, that gift of gab. Or maybe I don't want to see anything I've confessed. Maybe it's just simple shame that has me avoiding the backs of these.

But I went and read the last one I wrote a second time, and it's got me thinking about life. Memories. How we piece it all together. It's not in order, is it? My life feels like a shattered mirror, little shards reflecting me back but all jumbled and overlapping.

Sometimes I feel like I was sent to war before I was even a teenager, like those better years came later and my past is all buried beneath it. Sometimes I think Hope was in my heart before Anna, like she came first. I get it all mixed up. Need to shuffle the deck.

Or stop reading what I write. Set it all down and don't look back. Worked so far.

Mike.

That damn secretary of yours is here again, with her fake nails tappity-tapping. Where was she when you needed burying, huh? Fat load of use she is to me now, giggling outside my door.

Jesus.

In all honesty, Michael, I forgave you a long time ago. Well, not forgave, per se. It was more that I got past caring. Yes, that's it. I couldn't bring myself to care. She would've felt that way too, eventually.

What? You didn't think I knew? Babe, come on, let's not kid ourselves. Discretion was never your thing.

I was going to divorce you anyway.

Rita

PLACE STAMP HERE

TO:

Confession: I used to be a very jealous person, Rita.
Like... you wouldn't understand probably, but I could feel m
blood boil when I thought of another man touching my
woman when I was away. Heat would crawl ~~through~~
over every square inch of my skin like I was burning
up, and my scalp would sweat. Just the thought of it.
I could do that to myself if I wasn't careful, let
the thoughts sneak in and mess with my head.

I don't think I'm like that anymore.
For one, there's no one to be jealous ~~of~~ over.
Nobody has anything anymore.
I think I take some comfort in that. I'm
glad they're dead, the people who had
so much more than me. It's something
I take pride in. I made it to today,
and they're all in
the bellies of
maggots

[illegible] after
all.

Dear Clayton,

Are you there, my faraway friend, or have you joined the
anks of the dead? Either way, I bring news.

I see them, Clayton, in the fog. I've been watching from my
Window and I see them, lots of them, dark outlines in
heavy, stolen pelts, their teeth sharpened, their claws
eady. They're laughing at us, Clayton. They think of us as fools,
as easy prey.

They don't see me, though. I'm too clever for that. Stay low, stay
quiet, that's the key.

Shhhh.

I have a plan, Clayton. When they spring my trap I'll get them,
ust you wait.

Wait, wait, wait.

You'll be good at that by now, I expect.

Waiting.

Never doing.

Never mind. You wait. I'll do it
myself.

Rita

PLACE
STAMP
HERE

TO:

So it's not just me then. You've seen 'em too. I've killed so many of those things, Rita. I've wondered at times if they were even real. Maybe I was going mad, or trying to justify shooting them if they were people. I've done that before. Pretended people were something else so I didn't have to feel bad.

There's two kinds of fog in this world, Rita. There's the kind making it fucking impossible to get to you today. And there's the one we've been living in since the day we were born.

Confession: I think I like today's fog better somehow. At least I can see it.

Dear Clayton,

hope you find this message, and that it finds you in good shape. Not sure how much sense I've been making lately. Are my postcards getting to you? I've sent hundreds, thousands, perhaps.

believe it's 3 or 4 days since I last wrote to you.

It could just as easily have been longer). I'm afraid I'm not doing so well. But I shall keep sending my words out into this sorry world of ours until my last cylinder of gas runs dry.

For what it's worth.

Fact is, my leg is pretty banged up. I appear to have developed an infection and, frankly, it's kicking my ass. I found some antibiotics, which have helped, and my thoughts are somewhat clearer now. God willing, I'll heal.

Send good vibes.

Rita

PLACE STAMP HERE

TO:

There she is. I can see the Costco sign over the highway sound barrier. It's a risk, pushing in a straight line. Life is risks. Think I'll set out at first light. Something to take care of first.
Probably think they're safe, setting up a campfire in the middle of the road. Think their numbers will save them. I think they're coming for you, Rita. You don't know how lucky you are that I'm out here, watching over you, keeping them from finding you first.
Gotta go now. Five things to do.

Updated List of things I miss:

- Rooftop hot tub (plaster cast + water = smush)
- Music played LOUD (must work on that one. Why tf am I even hiding anymore?)
- Knowing I'm alone (yeah, that was kinda nice)

Updated List of things I don't:

- Hallucinations (not fun)
- Hangovers (solution: day drinking)
- Mike (still)

Not dead yet, Apocalypse.

Rita

PLACE STAMP HERE

TO:

That was the most beautiful thing I've ever seen. Right after dawn, the sun trying with all its might to get through, the underside of the fog crimson and gray. It lifted up from the roof, a small green balloon. I watched it through my scope to be sure. Must've just left your hands. I can picture you there, hopping around on crutches and cast, sending me a note, a beautiful smile on your face.

The golden hour, we used to call it. This time of day. Wish it could last longer.

Tucking this away knowing it might be the last time I write before I'm talking to you in person. Voice to voice. Man to woman. For real this time.

~~I love you~~

Clayton

Hi Clayton. A quick update -

- The customer wheelchair is possibly the best invention ever. Not up to time trial speeds, but an improvement on dragging myself backwards along the floor.
- No further break-ins as yet, so my trap still stands. Not sure what they're waiting for. A heavy fog, probably.
- Your postcards brighten my day. The one I keep under my chair cushion, to read when I wonder if I imagined you, the one that hangs tantalizingly from a tree outside, and the many I see in the sky, passing by. Send more so I might catch another?
- I'm all out of antibiotics.

Rita

PLACE STAMP HERE

TO:

I've got your antibiotics! Should have reached you today, but ran into some trouble. Figured it was one of your traps at first, but probably older. At the edge of the parking lot. Didn't get me but got me spooked. I think I know why you've been able to hold out so long: getting through these cars is a minefield.

Sleeping in a FedEx truck tonight. No windows in the back, so I can set up my light. Would make a good campsite, this. And if the gasoline hadn't all gone bad, we could take the puppy on the road.

Most of the packages here have been rummaged through, nothing much of use. But I found a book in the clutter. I'll bring it to you. Tomorrow. You won't see all these broken promises, but I'll tell you about them. I'm going to confess everything to you, my dearest Rita. It feels so good, writing it all down. Even better to say them.

Dearest Clayton,
While I had hoped you might find me, and that the infection in my leg might resolve, I fear neither will come to pass. It is therefore time for me to do what must be done. Were you to arrive too late, all that was mine is yours. Take this postcard as notification of my bequeathment. Enjoy it. I'd sooner it go to you, my friend, than to the sons of bitches out there. I'll do what I can to clear the way for you. If not all, I'll take down as many as I can. You have my word on that.
I'm not getting better, Clayton. The nightmares have returned and how much longer I can be of use is anyone's guess. Please don't feel bad, this is what I need to do, and believe me when I say, if I'm going out, it'll be in style.
Safe travels.

All my love,
Rita

PLACE
STAMP
HERE

TO:

Universe,
This may come as a shock to one as ancient as you, as all-encompassing. In fact you might want to sit down for it.
Ready?
You do not get to break the likes of me. I cannot and will not be broken. Do you know who I am? What you've created in me? Do you have the faintest idea what I am capable of?
Clearly not.
Oh, but I know you, all too well, and I won't play your game anymore.
That's what you cannot stand, isn't it? Not being deified?
You prefer us to be in a constant state of awe, on our knees, in the dirt.
Well, fuck you, Universe. This is on my terms, now.
Do your worst.

Rita

PLACE STAMP HERE

TO:

____

____

____

FAO: Fog Demons.
You are cordially invited to attend Racing Rita's Season Finale Party.
"If this store's rockin, ya best come knockin!"

Tonight.
After dark.
Follow the sound of disco.

I'll be waiting.

Rita

P.S. Bring your karaoke A-game, you big beautiful hairy bastards.

PLACE STAMP HERE

TO:

1/3

Clayton. It's Rita. I'm in trouble.

This won't all fit on a single card, so I'll have to make a set of 3.

My plan was to entice them into the store, get them to the warehouse where there's a huge lockable cage, then burn the fuckers to the ground.

I was very, very wrong, Clayton.

They're smart, way smarter than I gave them credit for. They knew about my trap (that's why they stayed away) and they were working out the best way to get in to avoid being caught.

Thank Christ for the wheelchair or I'd never have made it out.

(Cont...)

PLACE
STAMP
HERE

TO:

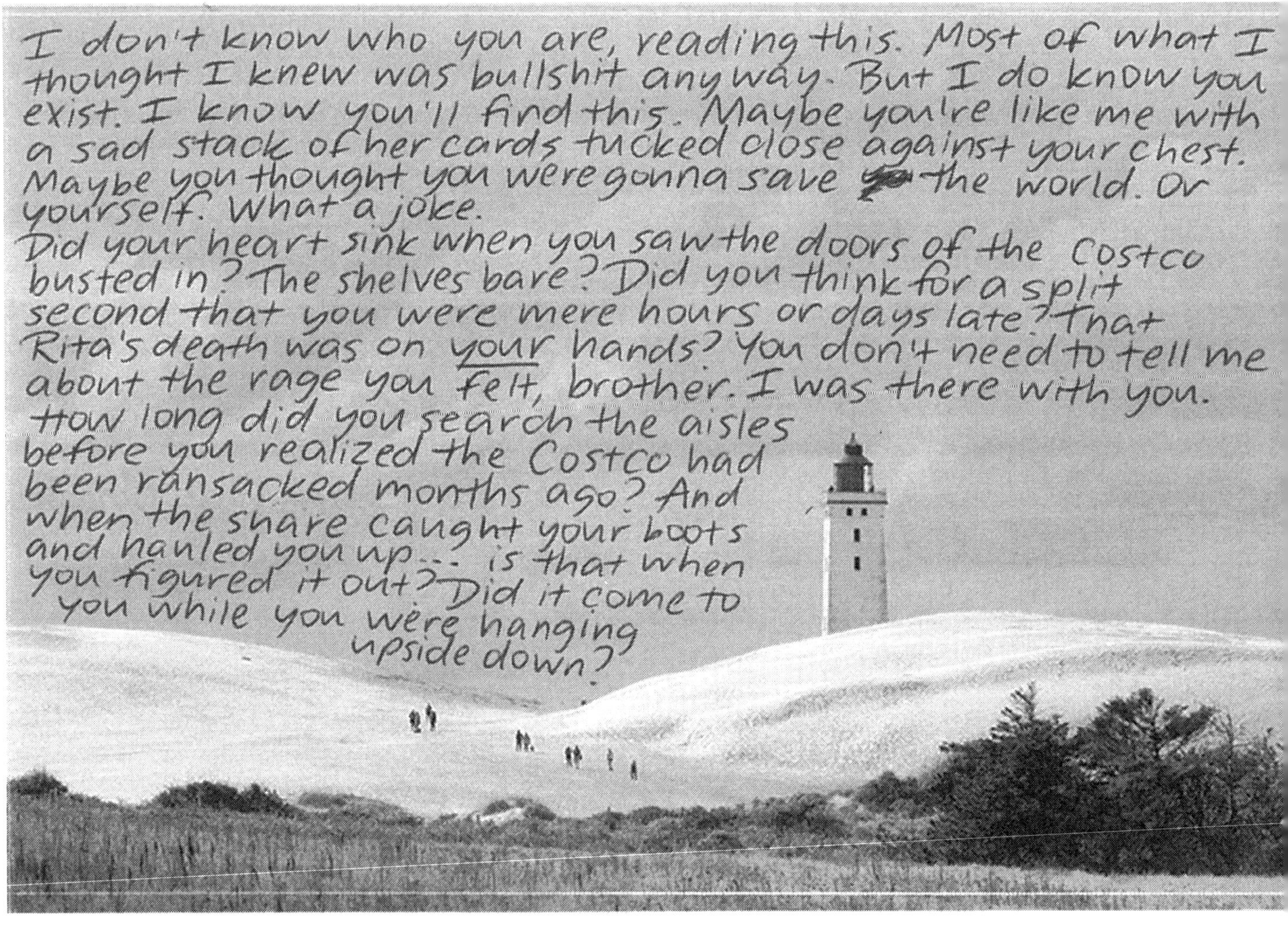

I don't know who you are, reading this. Most of what I thought I knew was bullshit anyway. But I do know you exist. I know you'll find this. Maybe you're like me with a sad stack of her cards tucked close against your chest. Maybe you thought you were gonna save the world. Or yourself. What a joke.

Did your heart sink when you saw the doors of the Costco busted in? The shelves bare? Did you think for a split second that you were mere hours or days late? That Rita's death was on <u>your</u> hands? You don't need to tell me about the rage you felt, brother. I was there with you.

How long did you search the aisles before you realized the Costco had been ransacked months ago? And when the snare caught your boots and hauled you up... is that when you figured it out? Did it come to you while you were hanging upside down?

I tried to hold them off, threw everything I could at them, but there are just too many, and they're so much stronger than I am. They've trapped me in the staffroom. Christ knows how I managed to get up the stairs with my leg as bad as it is. Amazing what's possible with the right motivation, don't you think? The door won't hold forever. A couple of them are taking turns barging at it, weakening it, bit by bit. I'm scared, Clayton. Really scared.

Look, I shall tell you what I know, then release these final cards on a balloon out of the window (fingers crossed they head the right way). What you do with the knowledge is up to you.

PLACE STAMP HERE

TO:

(Cont...)

I loved her too. The idea of her. I'm sure we all did. The cage stinks of their blood and bowels, all those who came before me. And now here you are, finding my little tin box among the detritus of the dead. A jackpot of Rita's missives. Nearly a hundred that I shot out of the sky, risked my neck for, chased across half a county to get to the source of.

He won't say a word, the fucker who did this. Not sure what he's waiting for. Working up an appetite? Waiting for my skin to loosen a little? I'm not even scared. Just tired. Heartbroken. And thinking of you, all the other saps out there I was worried would get to her first. I was just like you, wasn't I? Dumb. A danger to myself.

I see him at his desk right now, scribbling away, six canisters of helium and jumbo packs of balloons. If I could get my hands on one and send it between these bars, I wonder what I'd say to warn you...

PLACE
STAMP
HERE

TO:

____

____

____

Dear Apocalypse,

I'm writing in my capacity as sole survivor to inform you that, despite your best efforts, I'm still here. As you can see, nothing you've thrown at me to date has been enough, and I rather feel you have let yourself down. Try harder.

By my calculations I have enough supplies to last until my 127th year, so might I suggest you shift things up a notch before I die of old age, or boredom, or both?

From this rooftop I raise a vacuum pack of cocktail sausages and a beaker of warm chablis to you. Bonne chance. Bring it on, loser. Bring it on.

I await your response.

Sincerely,
Rita

PLACE
STAMP
HERE

TO:

Printed in Great Britain
by Amazon

29793939R00077